MR. JULY

HEROES OF ROGUE VALLEY: CALENDAR
GUYS
BOOK 7

ANN ROTH

Copyright © 2021 Ann Roth

Published by OliverHeberBooks

9781648396540

OLIVERHEBERBOOKS

Copyright © 2018 Ann Roth

Published by Oliver-Heber Books

0 9 8 7 6 5 4 3 2 1

 Created with Vellum

INTRODUCTION

Welcome to Ann Roth's exciting new series, Heroes of Rogue Valley: Calendar Guys series. *Twelve months, 12 gorgeous firefighter heroes and the women who steal into their hearts and forever change their lives.*

Meet Mr. July:

Summer Putnam's trust issues with men began during her childhood, and everything she knows about handsome firefighter Tony Clark reinforces that mistrust. Beautiful Summer is way too uptight and controlling for Tony, who has issues of his own. When a run of bad luck pushes them together, everything changes. Suddenly they're seeing a lot of each other. Their growing intimacy threatens to unravel Summer's rules for survival and overpower Tony's wariness of her. Can they overcome the scars of the past and open their hearts to love?

Mr. July—Tony Clark
   Age 30, 6'1" tall, 180 pounds
   Single

Proud Senior Firefighter
Time with Guff's Lake Fire Department: 10 years

1

Nothing more exciting than waiting in the bar line after a wedding reception—except maybe reading through new tax regs. Summer Putnam had been inching forward for what seemed forever. She wanted a fresh glass of champagne, and keep them coming. Under normal circumstances she preferred a sharp, clear mind and a firm grip on her self-control. Tonight, she just needed to forget.

Because wedding aside, this had been a rotten day. *Don't think about that now.* With determination, she raised her chin.

The woman in front of her, who had dark brown hair and was much shorter—in four-inch heels, Summer measured nearly six feet tall—turned to her. "I've never been to a wedding on a Friday night. What a great way to start the weekend, and such a beautiful ceremony."

Now there was something to smile about, and Summer did. The bride's dress, the vows exchanged, young William, Sam's son, beaming as he handed the rings to Sam and Adam... "It was awesome."

"The Carlson Hotel is the prefect venue." One of a

handful of hotels several miles from Guff's Lake, the hotel offered a large space for celebrations.

"Very classy," Summer agreed. As a whole she enjoyed a wedding, as long as it wasn't hers. "I'm sure Sam and Adam will live a long and happy life together." Which put them in the minority of happily married couples Summer knew.

"Are you a friend of Adam or Sam?" the woman asked.

"Sam. I do her taxes. You?"

"Also Sam. I met her in a knitting class when she and Adam were first getting to know each other. I had a hunch you were Summer Putnam. I'm Becca Chambers."

"How do you know who I am?" Summer asked after they shook hands. "I don't believe we've met." She excelled at remembering names and faces, a skill she'd worked hard to hone.

"Your hair is white-blond and you have the body of a model. You're every bit as stunning as Sam described."

Looks-wise, Summer didn't think she was half bad. But stunning? "Wow. Thanks."

"Your hair is so smooth and sleek. Who's your stylist?"

"Wanda Lipmann, the owner of Tommie's Hair and Nails. She's here—somewhere." Summer glanced around. "I don't see her, but she's wearing a fawn-colored dress, and she's with Gus Viggio. Big, handsome guy."

"Oh, I know who Gus is." Becca fanned herself. "Mr. March."

A color photo of the super hot firefighter appeared above March on the Guff's Lake Fire Department calendar. Each month featured a different man, twelve of the most gorgeous males on the planet. All proceeds went to the benefit fund, which provided monetary assistance to those who had lost their homes or possessions in a fire.

"I really don't know Gus at all," Summer clarified. "We met for the first time when Wanda introduced us after the wedding."

"I wouldn't want to bother her tonight. I'll give her a call her next week. I've been on the lookout for you. I need a CPA and you come highly recommended."

Summer was proud of her degree and her career, despite what had happened this afternoon. But she wasn't going to think about that tonight, let alone tell anyone. Too soon and too embarrassing, even if none of it was her fault. "What kind of business are you in, Becca?"

"Retail. I own Second Hand Rose."

"I know that store. I've bought furniture there. I don't have any business cards with me." Why carry a card for a job that no longer existed? "Give me your contact information, and I'll call you."

Becca gave her a card, and then, nearly at the front of the line, zeroed in on the bar. Summer tuned into the conversation behind her.

"I can't believe Hallie Sawyer caught the bouquet!" said a woman with a perky voice. "She doesn't even need it. All she has to do is crook her finger at Owen and he'll marry her. Mr. April—I wish he liked me."

"He doesn't even know you," her friend said. "Wish it'd been me catching that bouquet. I'd marry any of the available firefighters."

Summer smirked at that one. She didn't trust easily, especially men. As a rule, they tended not to stick around. Her mother, aka Shelley, had never had a lasting relationship, not even the marriage to Summer's dad. Her sister, Rainy, also had been through the wringer with the fathers of both her children.

Summer had been more careful in her selection of who to trust with her heart. She and Lee had been completely in sync, both ambitious to climb the corporate ladders of their firms. They understood the need to work long hours and had agreed to put off having children—if they had any at all—to attain their goals.

He was everything she wanted in a man, hardworking, monogamous, and loyal—or so she'd believed.

Wrong.

She cringed at the memory. For all they'd had in common, in the end he was no different than the other men she'd known. Love was unpredictable, and the consequences of falling in love painful.

So, no thanks.

The conversation behind her was still going strong.

"Did you see how Sam and Adam looked at each other when they danced that first dance together as husband and wife?" Perky Voice commented. "I've never seen two people so ready to be married."

"And little William, all smiles at having a new daddy," her friend replied.

Having never met her own father—her parents' shotgun marriage had ended before her mom had given birth and her father had disappeared—Summer understood the little boy's joy.

Perky Voice again. "Isn't it nice that Sam's parents are staying in town to take care of him while Sam and Adam honeymoon in Acapulco?"

"Yes, and I'm happy they rented this space until midnight. We're going to party hearty!"

Summer intended to take advantage of that, eating, drinking, and dancing her heart out. Then she'd go home and fall asleep instead of licking her wounds and facing the doubts and what-ifs. Plenty of time for that tomorrow.

"I hope one of the single firefighters asks me to dance," Perky Voice said. "If not, I'll do the asking."

"Who's your first choice?"

"I wouldn't mind dancing with Tony Clark—Mr. July. He's such a hottie, and I've heard he's a very good lover."

"Where did you hear that?"

"From a friend who knows a woman who slept with him."

"No way!"

Unable to resist that one, Summer turned to them. "I know Tony." Sort of.

The woman, who looked as perky as she sounded, widened her eyes. "You dated him?"

"No, but we've met." Once. "His mother introduced us. I handle the taxes for her business." Correction: as of this afternoon, she'd *formerly* handled Mrs. Clark's taxes.

"Way to get noticed. Are you interested in him?"

Summer smiled as if she might be, and on a physical level, she was attracted. But as good-looking as Tony was, he didn't seem to have much ambition to rise in the ranks of the firefighters. She wasn't interested in a serious relationship, but she still preferred the men she dated to share her drive to succeed.

A drive that pushed her to get ahead by climbing the corporate ladder. Being a plain-vanilla CPA had been all right for a while. But after seven years on the job and a promotion to first-level manager, she was eager to join the ranks of senior management, the next step to making partner, her dream since first joining Tillinger Morrison Evans, known by all as TME.

Instead, to her shock, she'd lost her job this afternoon.

Laid off!

The taste in her mouth turned bitter with disappointment, anger, and yes, hurt. She stifled a grimace. "Enjoy your evening," she said, and stepped up to the bar. "A glass of champagne, please."

"You bet."

The bartender, cute and about twenty-five, some five years younger than she, eyed her with interest. She was used to that. Men found her attractive. In that way, she was like Shelley. They shared two attributes. Their looks—same fair skin, thick, white-blond hair, and nut-brown eyes—and a love of pretty clothes. There the similarities ended.

Summer owned a house. She had an advanced degree, no unwanted children, and money in the bank, and thank God for that.

And where had the goal-setting, discipline, and hard work gotten her? Two months' salary in severance pay and a promise to give her a glowing recommendation.

"You look awful sad," the bartender said. "How about two champagnes, one on the house."

Summer flashed a big smile. "I'll take it."

Mello, the jazz fusion band hired for the evening —Ethan Goldberg, the sax player, was a firefighter and a musical phenomenon as well—had opened with the usual first husband-and-wife dance. Soon after, eager to catch their flight out, Sam and Adam had left and the band had taken a break. Any minute now, they'd start up again.

Summer wanted to dance, but first things first. She'd take the drinks, then find a table.

"YOU SEEM BUMMED," Nate, Tony's good bud and crewmate, commented as they ambled toward the bar after the wedding. "Bad date last night?"

Tony shook his head. "I went for a run with Boomer and turned in early."

"Man, your mojo with the ladies has been off lately."

No kidding. Tony hadn't taken a woman out in months. He was tired of shallow relationships, and go figure. Lately, even sex bored him. Talk about weird, and hell if he'd admit it. He should probably get a physical.

"You're awful good to that dog," Nate said.

Tony was crazy about his boxer, who asked for nothing but food and affection. In return, he was a loyal companion who didn't whine, nag, or complain, and often made Tony laugh. "He's a great animal."

"Who's going to walk him tonight?"

"Jenny has him until morning. He loves her." And no wonder. She spoiled Boomer rotten. Tony boarded him at her place Mondays and Tuesdays while he worked a double shift, forty-eight hours straight, at the station.

"Jenny's great," Nate said.

Best dog sitter in town. She'd once been married to Rob, a fellow crewmate. The ex-spouses weren't exactly close anymore, but got along well enough to co-parent their twin daughters.

"You never said what's wrong," Tony's bud added.

Plenty. A few hours ago, Tony's mom had dropped

a bomb. She sure knew how to pick the wrong time. He wasn't about to ruin the evening with bad news, or think dismal thoughts. He shook his head. "Tell you later. Nice wedding, huh?"

Nate grinned. "Adam picked a good woman."

"More like *she* chose *him*. Once she had him in her sights, he didn't stand a chance."

Over the last year, half the crew had paired up. Several were talking about following Adam's lead and legally tying the knot.

Seeing his crewmates pair up was both good and bad. Good that they'd found the right women for them. Bad that they were dropping like flies.

"Mello should start their set soon," Nate said. "See anyone you care to dance with?"

In serious need of a distraction from his mom worries, Tony looked around. Like a moth drawn to light, he homed in on the tall, willowy blonde at the bar. Summer Putnam.

She wasn't his type—too aloof, too no-nonsense, and too thin. He liked women with soft curves, who knew how to have a good time.

Summer leaned on the counter and chatted up the bartender, the flouncy skirt on her otherwise snug indigo dress hiking up the back of her thighs. And those silver, *do-me* stilettos...

Tony couldn't look away.

Also, she knew his mom.

"I think I found my dance partner." He left Nate and sauntered toward her.

She turned from the counter with a champagne flute in each hand, but seemed to be alone. "Is one of those for me?" he asked by way of hello.

"If you want it, it's yours." She handed him a glass,

her silver nails luminescent under the room's glittery chandelier.

"Cheers." He downed a healthy gulp.

Summer did the same. "This stuff is going straight to my head," she said. "I'd better eat something."

"Ditto that. Let's grab a seat first." He nodded at a table for two in the corner. "That looks available."

Seconds later, he hung his suit jacket on the back of one chair and draped a cocktail napkin over the other.

They were on their way to a huge, food-laden table on the opposite side of the room when Mello returned to the stage. The popular band had a big, local following. Before they played a single note, people headed for the dance floor.

"Do you want to dance first?" Tony asked.

"I'd rather eat."

After helping themselves, they returned to their table and sat down.

Tony eyed her heaping plate. A woman her size couldn't possibly finish half of it. "That's a lot of food," he said over the band's high-octane music.

"I haven't eaten all day," she replied in an equally loud voice.

"All day? Are you watching your weight?"

She raised her eyebrows. "Are you saying I should?"

"Hell, no." He let his gaze travel over her. She could use a few extra pounds, but he liked what he saw. "You look good. There are times at the station when I don't get a chance to eat, but I always make up for it later."

"I probably should have," she said. "But I couldn't."

"Why not?" he asked, curious.

Instead of answering, she stabbed a chunk of salmon and ate it with gusto. "This is delicious."

He'd never seen a female enjoy her food as much as Summer did. The women he gravitated toward tended to be more restrained. He hadn't expected her to be any different, but then, he didn't know much about her.

They'd exchanged maybe a handful of words when his mom had introduced them a few months ago. As usual, she'd wanted his okay before she hired a new tax accountant. Summer seemed serious and smart, and the firm she worked for had a decent reputation. He'd given his stamp of approval and then forgotten about her.

Busy with her meal, she didn't say much for a while. Again, different from the women Tony knew, and a nice change. He followed suit. Next time he came up for air, both their plates were half-empty.

"Do you always eat this much, this fast?" he asked.

"When I'm extra hungry." She nodded at his plate. "You aren't exactly holding back."

"Like you, I'm running on empty."

There the conversation, such as it was, ended. "I'll bet you're relieved to have the tax season behind you," he said.

"It's been grueling, but... I'd rather not talk about that."

Okay. "Gonna take any time off?"

She muttered something that sounded like, "More than I want to."

"What?"

"I scheduled my vacation for mid-June. A friend and I will be heading to Belize. We rented a bungalow near the beach."

"I've never been there."

"We went last year and had such a great time, we booked the same trip."

Was her friend male? Not that Tony cared, but he asked anyway. "Going with your boyfriend?"

"I don't have a boyfriend and I don't want one." She looked as if she'd tasted something nasty.

Having suffered through a few breakups himself back when he was young and stupid, he understood. "Ah, you're traveling with a girlfriend."

She nodded. "Dorie is my BFF. She's also a CPA, but at a different firm."

"What do you two do down there?"

"Sleep in, laze around, snorkel and swim, explore."

Visions of Summer in a bikini filled Tony's head. Sunning in a beach chair, tanning those long legs... "I'll bet you meet plenty of guys."

"Sometimes." She frowned at her fork and pushed the remaining food around her plate.

Making him even more curious. He wanted info but didn't press. "By the way, I'm not dating anyone right now, either."

No comment and not a flicker of interest. That shouldn't have bothered him, as he wasn't into her, either. Yet it did. Most women dug him. Why didn't she?

"When you get back from Belize, then what?" he asked.

"What is this, an interview?"

"Making conversation, that's all. You do taxes, but I have no idea what a CPA does the rest of the time."

"We're always working, but at a slower pace. In the summer months, we file corporate returns and late personal tax returns, and we focus on networking and bringing in new clients." She snorted. "A fat lot of good that does."

"Not your favorite part of the job, huh."

"The opposite—I enjoy talking with people and

I'm good at it. Last year, I brought in more new business than any of my peers."

She'd confused him. "You enjoy bringing in new business but for some reason, it didn't do any good?" She gave him a sharp look, and he shrugged. "That's what you said."

"Do firefighters ever have slow times?"

She didn't want to talk about her work. All right, then. "We're usually busy, if not with fires or medical calls, then with in-house training, conducting training for others, working out to stay fit, giving group tours of the station, conducting inspections... Stuff like that."

"Do you like what you do?"

"Yeah. The work is rewarding and I'm tight with my crewmates. Spending forty-eight hours straight together every week, putting ourselves in danger to save lives and structures, tends to bond people. They're like brothers."

Summer nodded. "As I recall, you're an only child."

"How'd you know that?"

"Your mother told me."

"She talks about me?"

"Every time I see her."

Tony wondered what else she'd said about him. Like that she wanted him to settle down, but never approved of anyone he dated? Not that he was ready by a long shot, if at all. "What about you—any siblings?" he asked.

"A sister."

"Is she a CPA, too?"

Summer shook her head. "She manages an eye clinic. We're as different as day and night, but I love her dearly."

She didn't say another word about her sister or

anything else, for that matter. Most close-mouthed female he'd ever met.

"Sitting at a desk isn't for me," he said. "I'm better with physical activities—fighting fires and growing trees."

"Growing trees?"

"I give them a good start, then sell them to nurseries." Tending the saplings relaxed him, plus he made good money. Thanks to his thriving enterprise he'd built up a decent savings.

"So you work two jobs."

"That's right."

"I had you pegged as man who puts his feet up on his days off."

People who didn't know him well thought he was laid back, a façade he'd developed as a kid to mask his fear and anxiety. Back then, he'd had plenty of them. "I'm not wired to put my feet up and twiddle my thumbs, but I do my share of taking it easy." His flute was empty. So was hers. "Still feeling buzzed, or would you care for a refill on that champagne?"

"I don't feel the alcohol at all. I definitely want another glass."

Him, too. Hanging with Summer was exactly the diversion he'd sought. Thanks to the packed dance floor, the line at the bar had dwindled to a handful of people. When Tony returned with two fresh bubblies, the empties and both plates had disappeared. He nodded his thanks to the guys bussing the tables.

Mello was still going strong. As soon as they emptied their flutes again, Summer pushed her chair back, stood, and smoothed her dress over her hips. "Now I'm ready to dance."

No doe-eyed glances or waiting for him to invite

her to the dance floor. She was a strong-willed woman, sure of what she wanted and going after it.

That side of her made him wary. One overbearing female in his life was enough.

Yet, unlike his mother, who'd pull just about anything to keep him tethered to her side, or had when he was younger and easier to manipulate, Summer didn't seem to care whether he danced with her or not.

Independent *and* strong, and not the least bit interested in him. Tony was intrigued.

Before he knew it, he was following her to the dance floor.

2

On the dance floor, Summer seemed like a different person. Not stiff and controlled, but vivacious and wild. The combination of food, champagne, and great music must've loosened her up.

What she lacked in voluptuous curves she more than compensated for with pouty lips, shimmying hips, swaying breasts, sexy stilettos, and great legs. Her fluttery skirt followed her movements, often baring a good length of thigh. Now and then he caught a flash of her panties. Fire-engine red. Talk about provocative.

She didn't seem to realize the effect she had on him, let alone guys on and off the dance floor. The way they looked at her, like starving wolves stalking their prey...

Feeling protective, Tony sent more than one narrow-eyed warning that made them avert their gazes. She may not think she felt the champagne, but her behavior said otherwise.

When they returned to their table a while later, someone had left them a fresh pitcher of ice water. Just what they both needed. Tony filled two glasses.

After emptying hers, Summer sat back. "That was

great fun," she said over the music. "I needed to let loose."

Mission accomplished in spades. Her cheeks were pink from dancing, and her formerly smooth, neat hair lay in disarray around her face. She looked uncharacteristically messy, but then, nothing about this woman was anything like the accountant his mother had introduced him to.

He wanted to reach across the table and tidy her up. Then haul her close and...

As if she'd read his mind, she fixed her hair.

Smart, competent, and hot, she could have her pick of men. Tony shook his head. "Why don't you want a boyfriend?"

"I'd rather focus on my career."

This came as no surprise. "A career is great, but there's more to living than work."

She sat up straight and gave him a sharp look, as if he'd touched a nerve. Before he could puzzle over that, she bounced the question back to him. "Why don't you have a girlfriend?"

No point dredging up the past with a woman he barely knew. "I like my relationships short and sweet, with no complications. I'll leave it at that."

They both went quiet and so did the band. It was awkward. Tony refilled the glasses. "You're not the only one who needs to let go tonight." At a sideways look from her, he blurted out the truth. "It's my mom. She might be sick."

"Don't tell me she caught the flu that's been going around."

Tony wished. "Something much worse."

"Oh?"

Summer seemed interested and he wanted to talk

about it. "A little history first. Back when I was in high school, she had breast cancer."

Dark times. His father, a salesman, had always been on the road a lot. When he was away Tony's mom had leaned on him, dubbing him the man of the house and all but smothering him with her neediness and insecurity. One night when his dad was home and had drunk a few beers, he'd admitted that her domineering ways were the reason he'd taken a job that required frequent travel.

With the breast cancer diagnosis, Tony's life had become a whole lot worse. Unable to handle her illness, dear old dad had stayed away for even longer periods of time. Leaving Tony, then sixteen, to deal with the after-effects of his mother's radiation, chemotherapy, and subsequent reconstructive surgery.

For seven long months, he'd juggled school with caring for her and working at Clark's Frames, the picture-framing business she owned. He detested framing pictures, hated giving up sports and girls, but he hadn't had much choice.

To his mother's relief and his, she'd gone into remission from cancer, thank you, Jesus, and had been healthy ever since. Until now. Maybe.

Between firefighting, the tree business, and other stuff, he had a full and busy life. Knowing how she operated, her worries could be a ploy for attention. Over the years, she'd manipulated him all too often with phony health scares. Heart problems (doctor's report: heart normal and healthy), kidney failure (kidneys normal and healthy), and a host of other life-threatening health issues that had proved false. So yeah, he was skeptical.

Except she'd never pulled a fake cancer scare.

What if this time was real? Dread made him swallow hard.

"I didn't know about the cancer," Summer said. "Look at her today—thriving, productive, and happy."

Tony wouldn't go so far as to say she was happy, but she did all right.

Summer looked stricken. "Please don't tell me the cancer has come back."

"She's worried it has."

"Oh, no."

"She doesn't know for sure. So far, it's just a feeling —her exact words when she told me this afternoon. Over the years she's had more than a few false alarms, usually when she wants more attention from me."

"That's harsh."

"But true. You can trust me on that."

"You don't spend much time with her?"

"We connect by phone at least once a week and have dinner together maybe once or twice a month. That's more than most thirty-year-old sons."

"My mother also likes to stay in touch, unless she has a boyfriend. Then she forgets all about me and my sister. Has your mom seen a doctor?"

"Not yet. She's going to make an appointment."

"Let's hope it's another false alarm." Her eyes twin pools of concern, Summer laid her hand over his. "Let me know, will you?"

"Okay." She was fine-boned, with a soft, warm touch. He imagined her fingers on a certain part of him. It started to get excited, but this was no time go to there. He slid his hand out from under hers. "I get the feeling you have your own problems."

"How did you know?"

"Lucky guess."

She blew errant strands of hair out of her eyes. "It's not important."

"Hey, I shared mine. Your turn."

"Maybe you should get us more champagne."

"Sure you want another glass?"

"If I'm going to talk about my situation, I do."

Minutes later, Tony rejoined her at the table with two glasses of bubbly. "So, tell me about what's going on with you."

She sipped from her glass, then sighed. "First, I need a promise that you won't tell a soul."

"I won't."

She gave a satisfied nod, leaned forward, and spoke in a low voice. "Earlier this week, I interviewed for a senior manager position at my firm—a step toward my goal of making partner. I was told that I had a strong chance of getting the promotion and that I'd find out this afternoon. Instead, I was laid off."

Not what he was expecting her to say. He frowned. "No way."

"I wasn't the only one. TME decided to downsize. They let all mid-level managers and a bunch of non-management accountants go. Half the company. The senior managers will stay on. If I'd received the promotion a month ago, I'd still be employed."

"That sucks."

"And it's scary. I need a new job, the sooner the better." She looked worried. "Don't say anything to your mother yet, okay?"

"I gave you my word. Why the secrecy?"

"I'd rather tell her myself. Tax season has just ended and I need a few days to adjust, then I'll call her and my other clients. After that, feel free to tell whoever you want."

"Got it. You're smart. You'll find something in no time."

"Cross your fingers. Darn it, I didn't want to talk about this tonight. My glass is empty and I want to dance again."

She stood. He wouldn't have minded staying put, but he wasn't letting her on the dance floor by herself. He rose and escorted her.

~

SUMMER HADN'T PLANNED to spend the evening with Tony, but after another round of dancing followed by a stop at the bar, they returned to their table.

The four-inch stilettos should've hurt her feet, but at the moment she felt fantastic. A strong indicator she'd had too much to drink. Her sober self disapproved, but her relaxed body and carefree attitude made up for the fuzzy state of her mind.

Tony played a big part in that. There was something about him, an irresistible urge to be near him. He seemed equally attracted to her.

Who cared if she didn't want to date him? Tonight was about forgetting her troubles and having fun, and dancing and sitting together filled that bill. He was also easy to talk to. The party was still going strong, and she wanted to spend it with him.

"Your eyes are an unusual color," she said, peering into the depths of his mesmerizing gaze. "Blue and gray with slashes of silver."

"My dad's are the same color. Denim blue, according to his wife."

Summer was confused. "I thought your father had passed away."

"Nope. As soon as my mom went into remission,

he divorced her and married his girlfriend. They live in Chino. Your eyes are a warm, golden color. Amber, I think."

"Actually, they're nut brown."

"Regardless what you call them, they're beautiful."

He looked both earnest and smitten, as if he wanted to sink into her eyes and maybe her soul. Summer barely restrained herself from looping her arms around his neck. Boy, had she overdone the alcohol. "No more drinking for me," she said. "I've had enough—way more than I thought."

"That's obvious."

"It is? Why didn't you stop me?"

"You're a determined woman. I couldn't stop you if I tried." He gave her a cockeyed grin and tugged at a lock of her hair, which for some odd reason made her ridiculously happy. "Don't worry, I won't take advantage of you." His smile reassured her. "You do need to sober up. Have another glass of water, then let's grab your coat, take a walk, and get some air."

She jumped on the idea. "Okay."

Moments after she finished her water, he helped her into her wrap.

"You don't seem exactly sober, either," she noted.

He grinned. "I'm buzzed, but nothing like you."

It was a clear, crisp April evening. Despite her lightweight dress coat, Summer felt cozy and warm. Although her feet didn't hurt, her toes felt cramped.

"I've been wearing these shoes all night and I can't stand them one more second," she said, holding onto Tony while she tugged one off and wriggled her liberated toes. "Ah."

He frowned. "It's too cold for bare feet. Plus, you never know what you might step on."

"Either I go like this or I don't go."

"Suit yourself, but don't say I didn't warn you."

Her feet flat on the pavement at last, she threw her head back and laughed.

"What's so funny?" he asked.

"Me, all dressed up and barefoot. I've never done this in public. Heck, I've never done it, period."

She started to fling her shoes into the darkness, but Tony stopped her. "You don't want to do that. Give them to me."

He stuck one in each of his coat pockets.

Summer wanted to melt. "That's so romantic."

"Okay. Is that good or bad?"

"Sexy." She covered her mouth with her hand. "Did I just say that out loud?"

"Yeah."

His eyes glittered with undisguised desire. Or maybe it was the streetlight. Either way, she wanted him. "Come here, you."

He lost the grin. "Easy, Summer. I'm trying to sober you up, not—"

"Ah!" Her left foot connected with an uneven square of sidewalk concrete, pitching her forward. Tony caught her, saving her from a nasty spill.

"You all right?" he asked, his hands firm on her upper arms.

"I don't feel a thing."

"You're bleeding."

Shocked, she glanced down at her foot. "So I am."

"Let's get back to the hotel where the light is better."

He put his arm around her and guided her there. To Summer's relief, he didn't let go of her, even after they reentered the Carlson Hotel. The accident had sobered her. She no longer felt the alcohol, but she was a little wobbly and needed his support.

The lobby was deserted, everyone still in the ballroom.

"My friend and I are guests of the Healey wedding," he told the woman at the desk. "She had an accident with a slab of concrete. I'm a firefighter and certified paramedic, and I need to clean up her foot and examine it for injuries. Do you have a first-aid kit?"

He flashed a dazzling smile, rendering the clerk awestruck. "I know who you are—Tony Clark, Mr. July."

"That I am."

The woman all but swooned. "It's in the back. I'll bring it right out."

Kit in hand, Tony headed to the women's bathroom.

"You can't come in here," Summer protested as he shouldered the door open.

"And yet, I did."

"It's a good thing no one else is in this room."

He sat her on the counter and frowned at her injury. "Let's get those toes washed and take a look."

After shedding his suit jacket, he rolled up his sleeves. Then he grasped her foot in his big, warm hand.

"I hope my polish didn't chip." She pulled her foot from his clasp. "What do you think of the color?"

Without stopping to study said color, he turned on the faucet and again reached for her foot.

"Wait," she said. "You didn't answer the question. Do you like this color polish? It's called Blushalicious. Sounds like a tongue twister, but that's what it's called. Blushalicious."

"Yeah, I like it. Now sit back and let me take care of you."

"I don't need any man taking care of me," she protested.

Ignoring her, he rinsed the blood off under the faucet. "Ow," she said.

"I'm almost done. That's a nasty scrape across your big toe. Swollen, too. Can you move it?"

"I think so—yes."

"Then it's not broken. I'll fix you up over there." He nodded toward the powder room furniture at the other side of the room.

She hung on tight to his biceps. So hard and muscled.

After he helped her into a chair, his eyes almost bulged out of his head. "You might want to adjust your dress."

She looked down. Her skirt hem had ridden up and her thighs were almost completely bared. "Oops." She tried to make herself decent, but failed.

"Here, let me." With a firm tug, Tony took care of the problem. "Now, relax and let me bandage that toe."

While he worked, she closed her eyes. He was both proficient and gentle, and he smelled good. Spicy and male—delicious. Summer felt something she hadn't felt in two years—desire. She wanted him closer. Needed him.

Had applying antiseptic ever been so seductive? His deft fingers enveloped the ball of her foot and all her toes in a gauze bandage, which he secured with tape. "That ought to hold for a while."

Not wanting him to move away, she did something totally out of character. Tugged on his tie, grabbed hold of his ears, and kissed him.

"Wow," he said, when she let him up for air.

Nowhere near ready to stop, she pulled him back down. "Let's do that again."

He glanced around. "Not here."

"Then get us a room."

"Are you serious?"

"I don't think I should drive tonight. Neither should you. I want to be with you and I'm guessing you want the same thing."

"That's the alcohol talking," he said, sounding like a stern parent.

"I'm happy, but nowhere near drunk. Otherwise, I'd never be able to say 'Blushalicious.'" She leaned in and kissed him again, letting all the heat and longing show. "Are you convinced now?"

As winded as if he'd sprinted around the building, he nodded. "I'm clean. And I have condoms in my pocket."

She hadn't even thought about birth control. Hadn't had sex in so long, she'd quit the pill and only lately had considered starting up again. "How many condoms?"

Growling, he tugged her to her feet and held onto her as she limped with him to the front desk. He set the first-aid kit on the counter, chatted with the woman from before, and handed over his credit card.

Moments later he grasped the room key. "You sure about this?" he said once they were out of the clerk's hearing range.

Summer *had* to be with him. Nothing else mattered. She nodded.

In the elevator on the way to their suite, they shared long, deep, passionate kisses. Her world shrank to Tony. His intoxicating smell, his powerful arms anchoring her close. Hugging his hips with her leg, his hand, sliding up her thigh, and inside her thong... She almost climaxed then and there.

When the elevator opened on their floor, he scooped her into his arms.

"I can walk, you know," she said.

"That foot needs a rest."

Snuggled against his chest, she undid the buttons on his dress shirt. "You really know how to seduce a girl."

He let out a low laugh. "You started it."

"I don't usually do this kind of thing," she admitted as he strode down the hall.

"That's cool. No, it's hot. Really hot."

He fumbled with the card key, opened the door, and stepped across the threshold. Like a groom with his bride.

She barely had time to register the thought before he kicked the door shut and carried her to the bed.

3

Sunlight poured through the window, waking Tony from a deep sleep. He hadn't even thought to draw the drapes last night. Beside him, a woman burrowed under the covers, with only the crown of her white-blond hair visible.

Summer.

Thanks to a shortage of rooms, many of them booked by members of the fire department and other wedding guests, he and Summer had taken the last available room, a suite on the fifteenth floor.

The windows faced Guff's Lake—no chance of prying eyes, and a good thing. The all-night fireworks between him and Summer had been private. As much as he'd had to drink, he remembered every red-hot detail. No hangover this morning, either.

Although she might.

Careful not to wake her, he slipped out of bed and closed the drapes, shrouding the room in soothing darkness. When his eyes adjusted he tidied up, collecting the clothes they'd discarded in haste.

His stuff lay in a heap on the carpet. Summer's bra, a skimpy red number that matched her thong panties, hung precariously over a lampshade. The panties lay on the floor, inches from her dress where she'd un-zipped and stepped out of it. Tributes to the lust that had driven them into a frenzy.

Tony set her things on a chair, then padded to the bathroom. After shaving and brushing his teeth, cour-tesy of the hotel's hospitality, he showered. He re-turned to the bedroom dressed.

She was still out cold. He passed through the bed-room and shut the door. Using the house phone in the luxurious sitting/dining room combo, he contacted room service, ordering coffee and breakfast for two, and a paper.

That done, he tiptoed into the bedroom again to check on her. No longer burrowed under the covers, she lay her side. Her face relaxed in sleep and one slender arm and creamy shoulder stretched toward where he'd lain, as if seeking him out. Her hair lay strewn across the pillow. She looked beautiful and sexy.

She was also passionate and uninhibited. Her wild enthusiasm had blown him away. He hadn't been turned on like that in a long time. Alive and burning and definitely not bored. Far from it.

And he'd assumed Summer was uptight and con-trolled. Never would've guessed she'd be the woman to revive his flagging libido.

She stirred and cracked one eye open. Looking startled, she sat up. Blanched and massaged her fore-head. "Tony. Did I—did we—"

His lips quirking, he nodded. "Several times."

"Then those weren't erotic dreams?" She groaned. "But I'm not on the pill. I remember telling you."

"Right. I wouldn't have sex without protection. We used condoms." All three of them.

"Thank goodness for that." She shut her eyes. "My

head is killing me. I thought I'd sobered up after the toe thing."

"Take these." He pulled a packet containing two aspirin from his pocket, then set a bottle of water on the bedside table.

"Thanks. Do you always carry aspirin with you?"

He shook his head. "I took it from the first-aid kit last night. In case your foot started to do more than sting."

"You washed it in the sink in the ladies' room."

"You were very brave. How does it feel this morning?"

She pulled her foot, still bandaged, from under the blanket and winced. "Worse than it did last night."

"I figured it'd stiffen up. After your shower, I'll take another look at it and put on a fresh bandage."

Glancing at the clock, she frowned. "It can't be nine-thirty. I never sleep this late."

"You did this morning. We didn't get up here until close to midnight and neither of us got much rest." Fooling around for hours, making love, talking and laughing, dozing, then waking up for more of the same didn't leave much room for zz's.

Despite her hangover and his empty belly, he wanted her again. Damn, he'd missed that feeling. He couldn't remember the last time he'd hungered for a woman this much. Not in a while. He was back to his normal, badass self.

Holding the covers to her breasts, she sat up and reached for the pain reliever. Color drained from her face. Clutching the blanket around her, she scrambled from the bed. "Excuse me."

She limp-raced for the bathroom and shut the door. Moments later he heard her retch. The toilet flushed and water hissed from the faucet. She stuck her head out the door. "Please hand me the aspirin and water, my clothes, and the cosmetics bag in my purse."

"What does it look like?"

"The purse is black satin. The cosmetics bag is orange with sparkles."

"Hang on."

She'd crammed enough stuff in the small evening bag—pen, paper, someone's business card, her cell phone, car key, driver's license, cash, and a credit card. At the bottom, wedged into the corner, the tiny, sparkly bag.

"Here are the things you wanted," he said handing everything over. A knock sounded at their door. "That's room service, with coffee and breakfast. I'll be in the other room."

After shutting the bedroom door, he let the server in. In no time, he settled at the table with his coffee and the paper.

He heard the shower starting, and for a moment he was tempted to join Summer. But they'd used all the protection. Besides, they needed to talk. He didn't want her getting ideas about him. Last night she'd told him she didn't want a boyfriend, but since then they'd had sex. Lots of it.

He was on his second cup of coffee when she appeared. Color had returned to her cheeks, and her hair was back to its usual smoothness.

"And it looks as if she's going to live," he teased.

"Barely. Remind me never to drink champagne again." She limped toward her heels.

"No shoes till I check that foot. Sit down and have some coffee. I ordered toast and omelets, too."

"I don't think I can stomach food, but yes to the

coffee. A quick cup—I can't stay long. I think my toe is okay." She sat down at the table.

"It needs to be checked."

"I'm fine," she insisted.

"Indulge me. If you're in that big a hurry, I'll do it while you eat."

She poured herself a coffee, then stretched out her shapely leg. He caught her slender ankle in his hand. Her toenails—what had she called the color? Blushalicious?—matched the seductive silvery shimmer of her fingernails.

Easiest thing was to rest her heel on his lap, but that was dangerous. He used his knee instead.

"Looks pretty good. All you need this morning is a regular Band-Aid."

"Told you. It must've really stiffened up—it stung something awful in the shower, and I can't believe how sore it is today. I hardly felt any pain last night."

"Something to be grateful for," he said. He was. Acute discomfort would've put a real damper on the love making.

"I must've been out of my mind to take off my shoes when we went for a walk. It's so cold this time of year."

"Hey, I tried to talk you out of it." Finished, he set her foot on the carpet. "All done."

"My toe and I appreciate the TLC. I can't believe I threw myself at you in the women's bathroom off the lobby and then asked you to spend the night with me." She glanced away.

"I'm not sorry. We both enjoyed ourselves."

She looked at him, the flash of heat in her eyes a compelling reminder of the unforgettable night.

What he needed to say faded into the background in a fog of lust. Not about to give her the wrong idea, he summoned the words back. "Last night was great, but I don't want you to get the wrong idea about us."

"I won't. It didn't mean anything. We... I needed..."

"You needed sex," he said. "We both did."

She blushed. Their gazes met and held, the tension between them hot and thick.

Averting her eyes, she reached for a slice of toast. "This was a one-time thing."

"Exactly." Relieved, he blew out a breath. "I want to see you again."

Had he just said that? "We have fun together," he hastened to explain. "In and out of bed."

Her brow furrowing, she pulled the napkin from under her juice glass and folded it in half and then quarters. "I don't know, Tony. I'm not into dating right now."

"I respect that you're an independent woman, and I sure as hell wouldn't want to mess with that. As I said last night, I'm not into serious stuff at all."

No comment.

"Do you mind telling me why you're not dating?" he pressed.

She got busy spreading jam on her toast. "It's not a pretty story."

"I still want to hear it."

"All right." She set the jam knife down. "Lee asked me to marry him. Several weeks later we flew to Maui to check out possible venues for the ceremony." Pausing, she bit her lip. "Then I caught him with a nineteen-year-old girl."

"Ouch."

"He ripped my heart to shreds."

Tony wanted to punch the bastard for that. "He had to be nuts to do that."

"I agree. I realize now that I was lucky to find out

who Lee really was before we married. Can you imagine what a mess splitting up would have been after? Returning the gifts, dividing up all those bills..." She started to make a face, then groaned and massaged her temples.

"Marriage is tough. At least it was for my parents," he said.

Summer nodded and nibbled on her toast. "My mother married my father because she was pregnant with me. He left before I was born. She's been involved with so many men I've lost count. Her longest relationship lasted less than a year."

"My parents were married eighteen years—I was born a year after they married. If they loved each other, they didn't show it. Even when I was little, when my dad came home between sales trips, things were tense. Getting into a serious relationship is one big crapshoot. I've tried a time or two. Charlotte, my last girlfriend... Really bad."

"Did she cheat on you?"

Tony shook his head. "She needed more than I could give." The relationship had started off well enough. Then and for no reason he could see, she'd changed into someone he didn't recognize, her constant demands for attention and reassurance impossible to satisfy. God knew, he'd tried.

Things had grown steadily worse until he'd thrown in the towel and split up with her. In hindsight he realized she'd depended on him like a crutch she couldn't survive without. Not all that different from his mother.

Since the breakup he'd steered clear of romantic commitments and was better off for it.

"I agree with you—relationships are risky at best. I haven't been with a man since Lee, and we broke up two years ago. What happened last night... The truth is, until now I've never had sex with a man I wasn't involved with."

That hadn't bothered her last night. Hell, they'd burned up the sheets together.

"When I decide I'm ready for a relationship, and right now I'm not, it has to be based on more than sex."

"I get that. Meanwhile, you have needs and so do I. As long as we're on the same page about what we want from each other..."

He let his eyes rove over her, gratified when she shivered.

But she glanced away. "I don't think so, Tony."

"Can't say I'm not disappointed."

"I need to go."

"Big plans?" He told himself he was making idle conversation, but he wanted to know.

"My sister Rainy and her boyfriend are looking for a bigger apartment—they're planning to move in together and her place is too small."

"Rainy, huh? Where'd she get a name like that?"

"She was conceived during a rainstorm."

"And you were conceived in the summer."

"You catch on fast. Anyway, while Rainy and Dayton look at places I'll be treating my niece and nephew to lunch and a movie."

"Sounds fun."

"It would be if I didn't have this hangover. I hope I don't run into anyone I know downstairs."

"That could happen. A bunch of couples who were at the wedding stayed here last night, including some of my crewmates and their ladies."

"I hadn't thought of that. We shouldn't leave together."

"Agreed. What we did last night is nobody's business but ours. I'll wait awhile before I head downstairs."

She plucked her shoes off the floor and sat down to ease them on.

Tony eyed the pointed toes and high heels. "Are you going to be able to walk in those things with your toe banged up?"

"I don't have much choice." She attempted to slide her injured foot into the stiletto, then gave up. "I think I'll go barefoot. It's a good thing the parking garage elevator is right around the corner from the lobby elevator. I'll race straight from one to the other."

At the door she paused and glanced back at him. "Thanks, Tony."

"For what?"

"Taking care of my foot—of me—and for breakfast."

"You didn't eat much."

"I had enough."

"Thank *you* for last night, and good luck with the job search."

"Oh, that. Don't remind me." She picked up her coat and purse, and opened the door. "Let me know about your mom."

Her dress whispered around her as she slipped out.

She was gone, but the faint scent of her perfume lingered. Underneath that, the smell of sex. Tony already missed her, but it was what it was.

He finished the last of the coffee, waited an extra ten minutes, then used the TV to check out. After making a final pass around the suite to make sure they hadn't left anything behind, he dropped the key card on the dresser and left.

~

CONGRATULATING herself for dodging people in the lobby, Summer made her way through the garage toward her Audi, careful to avoid grease spots and other debris on the concrete floor. As a whole, it was clean and well-kept, but you never knew, and in bare—

"Summer? Is that you?"

Summer stiffened and jerked her head up. Wanda and Gus. Lovely.

"You slept here?" Wanda said.

Her cheeks warmed and she knew she was blushing. She'd done that around Tony, too, and hated it. Why did she have to be so fair-skinned? She pulled her coat tightly around her dress. "I was in no shape to drive home last night."

"You look great today. Your hair held up well."

Gus glanced around. "Where's Tony?"

Talk about a nervy question. Summer managed a confused frown. "Um, is he still here?"

"Looks that way." Gus pointed out the forest green vehicle nearby. "That's his Mazda CX. Note the Guff's Lake Fire Department decal on the window and the personalized license plate. TC GLFF—Tony Clark Guff's Lake Firefighter."

"So I see," Summer said. Why couldn't they just continue on to their car and let her do the same?

"What happened there?" Wanda asked, nodding at the bandage on her big toe.

"I had a little collision with the sidewalk."

Gus's lips twitched. "That explains why you're carrying those heels."

"Did you break your toe?" Wanda asked.

"No, thank goodness."

Gus gave a sage nod. "I saw you and Tony leave last night."

Of course, he did. Summer wondered who else had noticed and who'd seen them enter the elevator together. "We needed fresh air, so we decided to walk around the block. We didn't get far before I had my accident."

Any minute now, Tony would show up to get his car. Wishing she'd worn a watch, she nodded at Gus's wrist. "Do you happen to have the time?"

"Ten-fifteen."

"If I don't hurry, I'll be late. Bye." Waving, she hurried away as fast as her limp would carry her.

4

By the time Summer changed clothes, slid her feet into a comfy pair of clogs, and drove toward Rainy's place she felt almost normal. If she made a sudden movement, her temples throbbed, but even that was fading. Aspirin was such a godsend. Makeup, too, and sunglasses, for shielding her eyes from the bright sunlight.

Best of all, she had no regrets about the night before. Her most sensitive female parts purred from Tony's delicious attention. She'd never been with a man so attuned to satisfying her. Before last night, sex had never been that great. She finally understood what all the fuss was about.

Which didn't mean she wanted it to happen again.

She'd intended to forget her problems for the night, and had. Now they flooded back. Jobless. The mere thought of unemployment made her feel queasy. She hadn't felt like this since before TME had hired her seven years ago.

Her childhood had been spent careening between feast and famine. The lean times when Shelley, Summer, and Rainy were on their own and had to scramble to find enough money for food and rent.

Shelley's solution had been to take up with one man after another, preferably someone with money, to take them in and bail them out.

When they were solvent, life was easier and more relaxed—at least at the beginning of a relationship.

But relying on a man—or anyone—caused a whole other set of worries and expectations. In return for paying the bills, Shelley's boyfriends expected deference and obedience. A setup doomed to fail, as all three Putnam women bristled under a man's thumb.

Of course, not all men were super macho like those Shelley seemed drawn to, but in general the ones Summer had known tended to leave. Depending on other people posed risks she preferred to avoid if possible. Taking care of herself was best. She'd put herself through college and secured the job at TME, earning a good salary that allowed her to eat out, enjoy annual vacations, and build up her bank account.

And thank God she'd saved. Two months of severance pay would stretch only so far, and who knew when she'd land a new accounting job? After she received that second severance check, she'd be eligible for unemployment benefits. Which would help, but felt like a handout—even if she had paid into the program since day one of her job at TME.

As Summer pulled into the guest parking at her sister's apartment building, she tamped down her worries. For the next few hours she intended to focus on her niece and nephew, and make this a fun day.

Loose shoes and a protective bandage on her toe only went so far, and she made her way across the parking lot at a slower clip than usual. Eventually, using the security phone, she rang her sister's apartment.

"It's Summer," she said, when Dayton, Rainy's boyfriend, answered.

"Come on up."

With a *click* the entry door unlocked. Summer usually climbed the stairs to the third floor, which took far less time than waiting for the tired elevator. But today she opted for the lift.

Compared to the spacious elevator cars at the Carlson Hotel, this one was small and shabby. She thought about the ride up to the top floor and plastering herself to Tony.

Thankfully, no other people had entered the car. If not for running into Wanda and Gus in the garage, no one would have even known she'd stayed the night at the hotel. Summer congratulated herself on convincing the couple she'd been alone.

Nothing to worry about.

The elevator shuddered to a stop at Rainy's floor. Exiting, Summer limped to the door. Dayton let her in. After dating Rainy several months, he spent most of his time here. With two small bedrooms barely big enough for the kids' twin beds and a foldout futon in the living room where Rainy slept, the apartment was too small and offered too little privacy.

Summer didn't care much for him, but her sister did. For that reason, she offered a warm smile. "Hi, Dayton."

As usual, his gaze flashed over her, too warm for comfort. Which was one reason she disliked him.

She didn't hide her disdain. "Where's my sister?"

"In the bathroom, doing what women do when they get ready to go out. Hayden and Maya, your aunt is here."

Hayden, age ten and way too cool to rush at Summer, sauntered over. Not so with Maya, two years younger.

"Aunt Summer!" she cried, hurtling herself into Summer's open arms.

For the first time all day, Summer smiled. When the girl let go of her, she squeezed Hayden's shoulder. "How are you, Hayden?"

"Hungry."

"Lately, you always are." Summer shook her head. "I swear, in the two weeks since I last saw you, you've shot up. You must be having a growth spurt. Where do you two want to have lunch?"

"The Rogue," both kids chimed.

The local restaurant, similar to Denny's, served the curly fries Maya and Hayden couldn't get enough of. Summer liked them, too. "I was hoping you'd choose that place. Let me say 'Hi' to your mom. Then we'll go."

In the bathroom, Rainy was adding mascara to her lashes. She finished and they exchanged warm hugs.

Like Summer, her sister had never met her father. The two of them had the same color of hair and wide smile, but there the similarities ended. Rainy wasn't as tall or fine-boned as Summer. She wasn't career-oriented, either, but unlike their mother who couldn't keep a job for anything, Rainy had managed the same office for ten years.

She narrowed her eyes at Summer. "You look amazing today."

"I don't see how that's possible." Not wanting anyone other than her sister to hear, Summer lowered her voice. "I'm recovering from a teensy hangover."

"I'd never have guessed. Your color is good and you don't seem to be suffering. There's a definite glow about you."

There was? Not about to share the reasons for the

happy hum in her body—after all, it would never happen again—Summer locked her lips.

Rainy crossed her arms and fixed her with a "Tell me" look.

"Hey, I'm dealing with a headache and a queasy stomach here."

Not about to let her off the hook, her sister lifted an eyebrow. "I'm sensing this is about a guy."

"I lost my job yesterday," Summer said, neatly pivoting the conversation in a different direction.

It worked. Her sister's jaw dropped. "What happened to that promotion that was a sure thing?"

"According to my boss, the company decided to downsize." Although Summer had nothing to do with the layoff, she was humiliated. Damned if she'd show it, even to her sister. She squared her shoulders.

"What are you going to do?"

"Find a new job." She couldn't be without work, not with mortgage payments and other bills. Tasting bile, she rummaged through her purse for a breath mint.

"You'll land on your feet. You always do."

"So do you."

"Putnam girls refuse to lose," they chanted in unison and high-fived each other. Just as they had throughout their childhood, whenever life at home grew extra difficult.

With that, Summer couldn't help but feel better. Although Rainy seemed subdued.

"I'm so caught up in my own stuff, I haven't asked about you," Summer said. "How are things?"

Rainy pivoted away to check herself out in the mirror. A moment later, she exhaled a major breath.

"Rainy?" Summer prodded, meeting her sister's eyes in the mirror.

With a sigh, Rainy lowered her voice and turned toward her. "Dayton and I aren't getting along right now."

This was the first Summer had heard about that. "Because?"

"It's a money thing. You and I both know how bad I am at managing my finances. Renting a bigger place is going to cost more than living here, which will put a big strain on me. Dayton earns almost double what I do. He knows how much I spend on my kids and our bills, yet he expects me to pay half the expenses on a new place. I don't think that's fair."

"Can you sit down and work out a budget that makes you both happy?"

"I don't see how, when he won't budge on what I should pay and I'm already stretched to the max."

"Are you sure you want to live with him? There's nothing wrong with changing your mind." Summer would send up a cheer.

"I have my heart set on looking at apartments, plus I like having a man around."

She sounded eerily like Shelley. Summer bit back the urge to go there.

"Dayton and I will figure this out. Back to your hangover. Did you take yourself to a bar or sit home and drink alone?"

"You know me better than that. I went to Sam and Adam's wedding."

"I'd forgotten that was last night. People do seem to pair up at weddings. I can't tell you how many times girlfriends of mine slept with guys they met at the party after the reception. Who is he?"

"Have you heard me say a single word about a man? Besides, what happens at the wedding..."

"Stays at the wedding. I knew you met someone!

Tell me it was one of Adam's hunky firefighter friends." Summer shook her head, but her sister pressed on. "Come on, I'm your sister."

"You should go into sales—you'd make a fortune. All right, yes, he's a firefighter, and don't you dare tell Shelley. Anyway, nothing will come of it."

"Which one?"

"Uh-uh. I've already said too much."

"Please, please, please tell me." Rainy's eyes widened, reminding Summer of when they were kids and her sister wanted something from her.

"All right, but not a word to anyone." After Rainy crossed her heart, Summer shared his name. "Tony Clark."

"Mr. July? Get out!"

"Stop, okay? We aren't going to see each other again." Summer checked her watch. "We should go. I don't want to rush through lunch or miss the start of the movie."

"That's all I get?" Rainy looked disappointed.

"Yep. Good luck this afternoon. I'll bring the kids home around dinnertime."

"No hurry. Tomorrow's Sunday and they can sleep in. Like that'll ever happen."

In no time, Summer arrived at The Rogue with Hayden and Maya. The restaurant was filled with the weekend lunch crowd. Families mostly and lots of kids.

"Do either of you see a table?" she asked.

"Over there!" Maya said, racing her brother to reach it first.

Ready to enjoy the rest of the afternoon, Summer laughed and followed them.

∽

As ALWAYS, Tony, his crewmates, and Captain Comings gathered at the firehouse table for breakfast Monday morning. Today's big topic of conversation was Adam and Sam's wedding.

"You really whaled on that sax, Ethan," Liam said, running his hand over his shaved head. "You and the band get better and better."

Nate nodded. "I wouldn't be surprised if someday you make it big."

Captain Comings eyed Ethan. "Anything I should know?"

"You mean, am I thinking about leaving the firehouse? No way. First and foremost, I'm a firefighter."

Satisfied, the captain went back to his breakfast. The conversation returned to the wedding.

"Wanda can't stop talking about the vows Adam and Sam exchanged," Gus said. "I liked them, too. Sam told Wanda she and Adam worked on them for months and neither knew what the other had written. Wanda wants to do the same thing."

Tony groaned. "Don't tell me you're getting married." The way things were going, he'd be the last single man on the crew.

"That's up to Wanda." Gus gave a goofy grin. "Rafe's next."

The dude nodded. "This fall, but don't expect an invite to the wedding. That'll be just her and me, her brother and his girlfriend, and their baby girl. You'll be invited to the party after."

"What kind of party?" Ethan asked.

"Something along the lines of Adam and Sam's."

Tony liked the sound of that. Maybe Summer would be there. Except she didn't do taxes for Rafe or Jillian—or anyone else right now. He tuned out the conversation and thought about her. Hell, he'd been thinking about her since she'd slipped out the hotel room door.

Worn out from their intense activities in bed, he'd slept like the dead Saturday. Last night he'd dreamed about her, hot, sensuous stuff that left him hard and aching but didn't come close to the real thing. *That* he wanted more of.

"Wanda and I ran into Summer in the hotel garage Saturday morning," Gus said.

About to shove the remains of a Samantha's Treats cinnamon roll into his mouth, Tony set it down instead.

"She was barefoot and still in her party clothes. Said she'd overdone the alcohol and had spent the night at the Carlson." Gus gave Tony a knowing look. "She didn't say who with, but that's obvious."

Across the table, Nate hooted. "One minute you and she were dancing, the next you disappeared. I figured something was going on."

"She looked hot in that blue dress," Owen said. "I don't blame you for getting a room."

May as well 'fess up. "She hurt her toe. I helped with that and we ended up in a room. It was a one-night thing."

Which didn't seem nearly enough. Maybe he'd call her. Not right away—he didn't want to crowd her— but in a few days. Since she'd asked him to keep her updated about his mother.

"She's not your usual type." Using his hands, Nate sketched an hourglass shape in the air.

"I got some bad news from my mom. Summer knows her from doing her taxes, so I started talking to her." He didn't mention that she'd lost her job. He'd promised not to.

Nate frowned. "You didn't say anything at the wedding."

"I didn't want to bum you out at the party."

"What's going on with your mom?" Nate asked.

His crewmates knew and liked her. Who wouldn't? On her occasional visits to the station, she brought them treats—pistachios, doughnuts, and great home-made sweets.

They were also aware of her medical history and the health scare stunts she pulled from time to time to grab his attention and keep him close.

He filled them in, and for the rest of breakfast the talk centered on her.

"When is she seeing her doctor?" Gus asked.

"She didn't say. Who knows if what she says is for real?"

Nate gave his head a somber shake. "Let's hope this is another false alarm."

Echoes of agreement followed.

"Stay on her to get checked, man," Rafe advised.

"Keep us informed." Captain Comings stood. "See you in ten."

Tony and his crewmates cleaned up the breakfast mess, then tromped en masse downstairs to the garage, aka the apparatus bay, where they met for the Monday morning meeting.

There, the captain started off with the usual—reviewing what needed to get done over the next forty-eight hours, delegating tasks, asking for updates on current projects, and handing out new assignments. Having recently finished a huge public safety project covering the urban, suburban, and rural areas surrounding Guff's Lake, Tony was ready for something different. He got it.

"Our annual community outreach and fundraiser

is in early June," the captain said. "This year we need money for a thermal imaging camera. A new jaws of life would be nice, too. Tony and Nate, I'm putting you in charge. I expect regular progress reports."

Talk about a plum assignment. The outreach event always proved to be a good time, with people from the community meeting the crew, enjoying the barbecue, and whatever else the guys in charge cooked up.

Totally onboard, Tony traded grins with Nate.

5

After spending Sunday putting a résumé together and combing through the help wanted-accounting ads online, Summer found a mere four openings locally for accountants. None of them management positions, but she couldn't afford to be choosy. With her laid-off peers sure to apply for the same positions, competition would be fierce, but she wasn't worried. Well, a little... Mentally crossing her fingers, she applied for all four jobs.

As she lay in bed later, her fears multiplied. What if she didn't find a job? What if she had to declare bankruptcy? How would she ever hold her head up?

Stop it! she ordered herself. Several times, for all the good that did. She spent a restless, fitful night.

By the time she gave up on sleep, the earliest of the early birds had begun to warble and chirp. Nursing a mug of strong coffee she sat the kitchen table and attempted to read the paper. Instead, she tormented herself with thoughts of the morning's inescapable task: clearing out her office at work. The thought of showing her face when she was no longer an employee... Shame washed over her. At least she wouldn't be the only one.

May as well get it over with. She showered and put on jeans and a T-shirt—no sense dressing for success today. After a quick breakfast, she headed for TME for the last time.

After parking and exiting the car, she dragged her feet, silently mourning what she'd lost. The lovely regular paycheck, the routine of spending Monday through Friday and sometimes weekends here, the work friendships, being part of a company she cared about and gave her all for.

She was going to miss all of it, even the boring meetings. Want to or not, it was time to move on. Holding her head high—she would not let them see her defeated—she entered the building. Already the atmosphere felt different. Gloomy despite the sunny atrium, the usual energy and camaraderie missing.

Monday mornings, the firm kicked off the week ahead with a mandatory, all-employee meeting. Which effectively excluded her and the rest of the laid-off employees.

Summer, and several of her former peers who'd also arrived to gather their personal belongings, commiserated before they separated.

Sucking in a deep breath she entered what her now former office, which she'd fondly dubbed her home away from home. She'd spent so much time here, over the years adding personal items to make it her own. Framed school photos of Hayden and Maya on her desk, the glass paperweight from a grateful client, the red vase filled with now-wilting spring flowers, the "I'm an accountant—what's your super power?" clock the employees who reported to her had given her one Christmas.

She was going to miss them and her clients as well, many of whom had also become friends.

Security had shut off access to the company database, a routine requirement when an employee left the company. TME didn't want her filching the accounts.

They didn't know about her client address book. She stuffed that into her oversize purse. The company had required her to sign a one-year, non-solicitation clause that had taken effect Friday afternoon and prevented her from soliciting any of the firm's clients for a full year. Regardless, over the next week she planned to contact most of them. As soon as the twelve months ended, she intended to woo them back.

For a moment, the thought buoyed her spirits. Then, like a punctured helium balloon, she sank low.

Hollow inside, she sat down at her desk for the last time and phoned Dorie. Weeks ago they'd made a dinner date for later in the week to finalize the details of their trip to Belize, but Summer had a lot to tell her BFF. Dorie didn't even know she'd been laid off. She didn't know about Tony, either.

She didn't pick up, no doubt at her own Monday morning company meeting. Well, shoot. Summer left a voice message. "Can we switch dinner to tonight instead of later in the week? It's important."

If Dorie wasn't available, maybe Tony was. He knew what had happened Friday, and Summer could use a friendly ear. They hadn't exchanged contact info, but his mom had given Summer his cell phone number. It was in her client address book. Summer looked it up and called him.

After two rings she changed her mind. She didn't plan to see him again, and it seemed best not to talk to him, either. Without leaving a message she disconnected. Moments later she received a text from Dorie. *Six o'clock tonight. Barclay's.*

"Oh, thank God," Summer said out loud.

Her friend would help her figure out the smartest career move. She might even have a lead or two. Feeling better already, she replied with a smiley face.

But dinner was hours from now, and she still had an office to pack up. Her personal effects fit into the boxes she'd brought along. Each ended up being heavy and she was trying to figure out a way to carry them together so that she wouldn't have to make two trips when Michelle, her former administrative assistant, knocked and poked her head around the door.

"I came to say good-bye. Do you need help with those boxes?"

"As a matter of fact, yes. Take one."

After they set the boxes in Summer's trunk, she bit her lip. "You've been the best possible admin. I'm going to miss you."

"Me too." Tears glistened in Michelle's eyes. "This is so sad."

Summer blinked back a few tears of her own. She didn't cry in front of anyone, a holdover from when her mother's boyfriend Norm had made fun of her and Rainy for crying when the sweet elderly woman up the block had passed away. "Weak little pussies," he'd taunted.

They'd been eight and five, too young to understand, but the tone of his voice had conveyed his disgust.

"What are your plans?" she asked Michelle.

The admin's attempt at a smile missed the mark. "Find a new admin job. How about you?"

"I've already applied for several accounting positions."

"I've been doing the same thing," Michelle said. "Good luck to both of us."

Summer held up her crossed fingers. "If you need a recommendation, I'm happy to give one. Let's keep in touch."

They hugged and went their separate ways.

As soon as the Monday morning meeting ended, Tony and Nate headed upstairs to the firehouse kitchen to make coffee and work on the community barbecue and fundraiser.

While waiting for the coffeemaker to finish, Tony checked his cell phone. And look whose name popped up on the missed-calls list—Summer.

"That's some grin," Nate said.

"Summer called."

"You said the other night was a one-time thing."

"That's what we decided. She didn't leave a message. Huh."

"She probably butt-dialed you. Or maybe she wants to see you again."

Not according to her. "If so, wouldn't she have left a message?"

"Beats me. I know better than to try and second-guess a grown woman. Hell, I've been divorced twice. How'd she get your private number?"

"My mom had me add her number to my address book when she hired Summer as her accountant. She probably made Summer do the same with mine. Coffee's ready."

"If you want to phone her back before we get started..." Nate said as they filled their mugs.

Tony was torn. If she'd changed her mind and wanted to get involved with him, great. But she'd lost her job, and the thought of her leaning on him to shore her up... He broke into a cold sweat. Between his mother and Charlotte he'd had enough of that to last a lifetime.

And he wasn't going to think about Summer anymore. He shook his head. "Let's get to work."

He and Nate sat down and brainstormed the community event. "We have the date and the venue—first Saturday in June at Orchard Park, same place as always," he said. The two-acre, in-city park was walking distance from the station, which was convenient. "We provide the hot dogs, burgers, and bottled water. People who attend are welcome to bring side dishes, but that's not a requirement."

Nate nodded. "Most everyone brings food anyway. How much do you want to charge this year?"

"Not too much, but enough to cover our costs. We want everyone in the community to feel welcome, regardless of their financial status."

"Agreed. We'll use social media and flyers to get the word out, and place an announcement in the *Guff's Lake News*. What about activities and games?"

They came up with ideas for people of all ages.

"Raffle tickets?"

"You bet. Otherwise, how will we pay for the new equipment we need? The winner gets a basket of stuff donated by local businesses. We'll need to make calls and solicit donations. We'll start with last year's list and build from there."

They were hard at it when the alarm sounded. Dispatcher Sarah McCone announced a fire call.

"We'll get back to this later," Tony said as he and Nate hot footed their way to the brass fire pole and slid down to the apparatus bay.

As the fire truck sped toward the fire, he pulled out

his cell and stared at it. Despite his best intentions to put Summer out of his mind, he hadn't.

"Gonna call Summer back?" Nate asked.

Gus hooted. "I guess the other night wasn't a one-time thing."

"Hey, she contacted me," Tony pointed out.

Screw it, he decided, and slid the phone back into his pocket.

6

After a nonstop day, Tony and his crewmates sat down to dinner at the big table in the firehouse kitchen. This was Rob's night to cook, and the guy served a wicked spicy meatloaf with mashed potatoes and other sides. Over the meal they rehashed the stubborn warehouse fire they'd battled earlier that afternoon.

"The back half of the building destroyed, business shut down for the foreseeable future?" Rob shook his head. "I feel for the employees and their families."

Didn't they all. "Things could have been much worse," Tony said. "Out of the hundred-plus workers in the facility, only one sustained a second-degree burn. Twelve suffered mild smoke inhalation, with two sick enough for a trip to the ER. We did all right."

"Just another day at the GLFD," Nate quipped, and the conversation shifted to other stuff.

After dinner, Tony headed outside to get some fresh air. Enjoying the clear, crisp evening, he strolled around the perimeter of the building. Next thing he knew, he called Summer. Because hey, he needed to know whether she'd tried to reach him on purpose.

No answer. "You phoned this morning without

leaving a message," he said in his voice mail. "Maybe the call was a mistake. If not, I'm around."

Inside again, he watched the tube with a couple of crewmates. She didn't call back. When he tumbled into bed hours later he was still thinking about her and wishing she was with him under the covers.

❧

DORIE HAD ORDERED a cocktail and was clearly savoring every sip. She frowned at Summer's soft drink. "Are you sure you don't want something stronger?"

"I'm off alcohol for a while."

"Since when?"

"Since I woke up with a hangover Saturday morning."

The salads arrived.

"But you're Miss Self-Control. In all the years I've known you—and how many umpteen years ago did we meet at a professional women's networking breakfast?—you've never been drunk. Not even after Maui."

"Because I know from all the breakups my mom suffered through that heavy drinking never helps heal a broken heart or anything else. And I wasn't drunk—I just overdid a little. I really needed to let loose, and alcohol made it easier."

"Define 'let loose.' "

"It won't make sense till you know what happened Friday afternoon. Unless you've already heard through the grapevine..."

"Heard what?"

She filled Dorie in.

Her friend choked on her drink. "Holy crap. No, I hadn't heard. What are you going to do?"

"Find a job." And try not to stress herself to death. "If you happen to know of anything..."

"We had one at Voorhees, but we filled it last week. I'll keep my eyes open. There are lots of accounting firms in town. Anyone would be crazy not to hire you."

"From your mouth to their ears... I checked the help-wanted accounting ads and applied for every one. There aren't many, and with the layoffs, competition will be stiff."

"If it were me, I'd cold-call all the firms in town."

"That's not a bad idea."

The evening was turning into a "poor me" party Summer didn't want to have. "Back to Friday night. You can imagine how upset I was. There I was, at Sam and Adam's wedding. I could have gone home after the reception, but Mello stayed and played at the after-party, and you know how great they are. I was going to drink my champagne, then head to the dance floor, but then Tony asked me to dance and—"

"Hold on. Who's Tony?"

Before answering, Summer glanced around. Being a Monday night, Barclay's was quiet and only half-full, but in the town of almost twenty thousand, you never knew who might be there.

Good thing she checked, because she spotted Betty Randall and a few of her gray-haired lady friends on the other side of the dining room. Too far away for most people to eavesdrop.

Betty wasn't most people. When it came to someone else's business, the sweet-faced, grandmotherly woman seemed to possess radar-sharp hearing. And a big mouth.

At the exact moment Summer glanced Betty's way, the woman raised her eyebrows as if sensing she was about to reveal a juicy story.

"Betty Randall is staring at us," she warned. Wearing twin smiles, she and Dorie waved. "She was at the wedding, but she left after the reception. I swear, the woman has a sixth sense for things that are none of her business."

"How else do you expect her to keep her reputation as the woman in the know?" Dorie murmured.

The waitress delivered dinner, and the conversation stopped.

"You were going to tell me about Tony," Dorie reminded Summer when they were alone again.

Over the meal, she shared everything she could remember, starting with their first glass of champagne and ending with her toe accident. Her friend looked more and more envious. She had a copy of the calendar and knew who Tony was. What female in Guff's Lake didn't? Even kids liked looking at the hunky firefighters.

"By then it was late," Summer went on. "Neither of us was in any shape to drive, so we checked into the hotel."

"You and Tony Clark, alone in a hotel room all night? OMG!"

"Keep your voice down," Summer warned. Yep, Betty was staring again. "I hardly believe it myself."

"Is he good in bed?"

"Good" didn't begin to define the man's skill. Summer's intimate parts began to hum and ache. "Let's just say, he's very detail oriented."

"Ooh."

"The next morning we agreed that what had happened was a one-time thing," Summer went on. "We'd no sooner done that, when Tony asked to see me again."

"This gets better and better."

"Not really—I said no."

"Are you nuts?"

"I have my reasons." Counting with her fingers, Summer ticked them off. "One, now that I'm unemployed, I need to focus on finding a job. Two, Tony is super laid back, and three, he has a reputation."

"You don't have to marry the guy. If you like him and he likes you, why not see each other? Not to be cliché about it, but he happens to be tall, dark, and yummy. Anyway, you already slept with him."

The sleeping had been minimal.

"He was honest about what he wanted and it isn't a serious relationship," Summer explained. "Which is good because I'm nowhere ready for that. But I told him that a relationship based on sex isn't for me."

"At least you were both straightforward, and right upfront. That doesn't always happen. You aired your differences and parted ways. What's the problem?"

"I can't stop thinking about him."

"Great sex will do that to a person."

Wearing a smile—how much had she heard?—the waitress handed them a dessert menu. "We have some excellent desserts tonight. If you're in the mood for chocolate, our devil's food decadence cake is going fast."

"We have to have that," Dorie said. "One piece and two forks."

As they savored the cake, Summer made a confession. "I called Tony this morning, but then I changed my mind and disconnected."

"So you are interested." With a gleam in her eye, Dorie licked her fork clean.

"Yes, but I don't want to be. Besides contacting a temp agency, what am I going to do about a job?"

"All right, we won't talk about Tony anymore. You

never know with temp jobs—sometimes they lead to permanent positions. And don't forget the Professional Women's Networking Association. You got the email about this month's breakfast, right?"

"A while ago. I deleted it."

"I'll forward it to you. This month's meeting is a week from Wednesday. Talk about the perfect place to announce that you're looking for a job."

"Can't hurt," Summer mused. "I haven't been to a meeting since the Christmas party last December."

"There you go." Dorie glanced at her watch. "It's getting late and I have to be at the office early tomorrow. Being laid off is no fun, but at least you get to sleep in."

Given the choice, Summer would gladly choose work. She signaled for the check. "We didn't get a chance to talk about you or Belize."

Dorie hesitated. "Do you still want to go?"

"I wouldn't miss it. Regardless what's happened, I need a vacay with my bestie."

"Aww. We both do. I'm not worried about the details. We've taken care of the big stuff—reserving the cottage and buying our plane tickets. We've been there before and know what to expect. We'll figure the rest out when we get there. As for me, things are the same as the last time we got together. Paul still doesn't know I exist."

Dorie had a thing for the property manager of the building where her accounting firm was located. They leased the top three floors. Paul's office was off the main-floor lobby and Dorie saw him daily.

"Why don't you invite him to coffee?" Summer asked as they paid the bill.

"Since he hasn't asked me, I might as well."

With May right around the corner, spring had arrived in full force. The days seemed to grow warmer by the week, but nights continued to be cool, and as they stepped outside, Summer shrugged into her lightweight coat. "This was fun. Have a good rest of the week."

"You, too. Hang in there, and I'll let you know if I hear of any job openings. If anything happens with Tony, I want to know."

"Ditto with Paul. Don't hold your breath about Tony. I don't plan to contact him again and I don't expect him to get in touch with me. But I will cold-call accounting firms and show up at that breakfast."

Dorie gave a thumbs-up. "You'll have a job in no time."

7

"Hell of a two days," Tony said as he and his crewmates clocked out Wednesday morning. "We got, what—three hours' sleep last night and six the night before?"

"At most." Max rubbed his red eyes. "I'm running on empty and jonesing for Rosemary's breakfast special."

Rosemary's Breakfast Nook was two blocks away from the station and the go-to place for strong coffee and dynamite food. Wednesdays, Rosemary reserved a big table for whoever showed up from the station.

"Are you coming with us?" Max asked.

Tony shook his head. "I'm gonna pick up Boomer, head home, and crash."

"I hear that. Megan's coming over tonight, and I need to rest up." Max flashed a big grin.

The dude sure had cheered up since he and Megan had become a thing.

Not a cloud in the sky this morning, making for a pleasant drive to pick up Boomer.

Birds twittered, squirrels scampered up and down budding trees, and the sweet smell of spring flowers scented the air. With weather this good, a man couldn't help but be happy. Whistling, Tony ambled toward Jenny's front porch. Even before he knocked at her door, Boomer gave a joyous woof from inside.

Jenny let Tony in. "He's been checking the door since breakfast."

Nice to be loved. Grinning, Tony bent down to greet the boxer, who licked his face and wagged his stub of a tail.

"Thanks for taking good care of him," he said as he leashed Boomer. "See you next week."

For all Boomer's ecstatic greeting, he gave Jenny a mournful look. She adored him and so did her twin high school-age daughters. The three of them spoiled him rotten. But then, they spoiled every canine in their care.

Finally at home, Tony made himself a PB&J sandwich for breakfast. He filled Boomer's water dishes both in the house and out back, then penned him in the fenced yard. With a dog house, shade trees, and almost an acre to run around in, his dog had no complaints.

In the greenhouse at the rear of the yard, Tony inspected dozens of potted saplings he'd nurtured from seed. With the danger of frost no longer a concern and the young trees hardy and healthy, they were ready for the great outdoors.

He spent a fair chunk of time loading pots onto a custom-made dolly and transporting them to a second fenced area, built to protect them from Boomer's curiosity. That done, he weeded and watered and fertilized—and thought about Summer.

He hadn't heard back from her. She probably had butt-dialed him the other day. Seemed as if she didn't need to lean on him, after all. Didn't want to see him for other reasons, either.

Ah, well. Win some, lose some.

Dead on his feet, he returned the dolly to the shed near the greenhouse, then plodded toward Boomer. "I need to get some sleep, Boom. You stay out here. When I get up, we'll go for a run."

As soon as his head hit the pillow, he passed out. He was dreaming about a three-alarm fire when he jerked awake. His cell phone was ringing.

His mother. He sat up and scrubbed the sleep out of his eyes. "Hey, Ma."

"I woke you. I'm guessing you didn't get much rest at the station."

"We were busy." He squinted at the clock. Almost three o'clock. He'd been in dreamland about four hours, plenty long enough. "No worries—it's time for me to get up."

Cupping the phone to his ear, he padded into the kitchen to make coffee.

"I'll bet you're glad to be home."

"Always." She hadn't told him the reason for her call. Was she feeling bad? Tony tensed. "You okay?"

"I'm doing all right," she said in her worried voice. "I wanted to let you know that Summer was laid off."

"How did you hear about that?"

"She called and told me. You sound as if you already knew."

"She was at the wedding Friday night. She told me then."

"That was almost a week ago, and you didn't think to mention it?" She sounded hurt.

"Summer asked me not to. She wanted to tell you herself."

"You let her know I might be sick."

"Was it a secret?"

"No, but I didn't expect her to ask about it. Seems

as if you and she had quite a conversation at that wedding."

"Don't read anything into it, Ma. Listen, I gotta go."

"Wait just a minute. I called because I want you to know that I took your advice and made a doctor's appointment."

"All right. When is it?"

"Friday at three o'clock."

"Why don't I come with you?"

"I'd hate to put you out," she said, using the petulant tone that had guilted him and kept him at her side since he was a kid.

Couldn't she for once come out and say what she wanted instead of playing guessing games? He rubbed his hand over his face. Scratchy. He needed a shave but wouldn't bother until morning. "I'll pick you up, okay?"

"Thanks. You're such a good son. What's that noise?"

"The coffeemaker."

"Decaf, I hope."

"Nope."

"It's after five. Are you sure you should drink regular coffee this late in the day? Between the caffeine and that nap you just had, you'll be up all night."

He was thirty years old and she still treated him like a kid. He barely masked his irritation. "I'll be fine, Ma. See you Friday."

After he drained his mug he changed into running clothes. Outside, he whistled for Boomer. He leashed the dog, and they headed off.

~

AS A RULE SUMMER avoided stop-and-go rush hour traffic whenever possible. Which should've been easy now that she was unemployed. But a trip to a temp agency across town had taken longer than she'd imagined, and here she was.

On the positive side, she had a job at an accounting agency. Answering phones wasn't exactly what she'd envisioned, but beggars couldn't be choosy and all that. The company's receptionist had been summoned for jury selection and they needed a replacement. The pay was terrible and the job only lasted two days—unless the woman was selected as a jury member, in which case Summer would stay until either she found a permanent position or the receptionist returned.

Idling in traffic was no fun, especially on a warm afternoon. Summer lowered all the windows. With the lush meadow grass bending gently in the wind and the sweet smells of spring in the air, she could almost forget her worries.

But not quite. Change had never been easy for her, especially when she wasn't sure where she'd land. Having her life up in the air was downright uncomfortable.

The savings she'd squirreled away was meant for emergencies. Unemployment qualified as an emergency of sorts, but the thought of tapping into her reserve scared her. Because when the money ran out...

She knew first hand what could happen then. How many times had the family been broke? Each time, her mother lost all sense of pride. Groveling, flirting—she'd do almost anything to lure a man with money into rescuing her.

Summer cringed. No thanks. She would never, ever depend on a man to bail her out.

Yesterday and this morning she'd cold-called a number of accounting firms, with nothing to show for her efforts, not even a nibble. She could always wait tables or work as a cocktail waitress. She'd put herself through college doing both.

Stopped at a red light, she noted the gloriously buff male running through the meadow alongside the road and couldn't believe her eyes—it was Tony and a handsome dog leashed at his side.

A dark T-shirt clung to his broad chest, which heaved with effort as his powerful legs pounded over the ground. He seemed to fly across the field.

The slowly sinking sun bathed him in golden light, as if he were a god instead of a mere mortal. Summer tapped her horn. He glanced over his shoulder, then changed direction and jogged over.

"Hey." Leaning down, he peered through the window. Sweat beaded his forehead. "I returned your call the other day. Did you get my message?"

She opened her mouth to explain that her call had been a mistake, when the light turned green. Behind her, a line of impatient drivers pounded their horns.

"All right, all right," she muttered.

"There's a place to pull off ahead," Tony said. "See you there in a few."

He and the dog took off running again.

When she pulled to a stop in the large dirt turnaround some moments later, they were waiting for her. *Always Ready*, the front of Tony's shirt proclaimed above a drawing of a fire hat and two crossed axes.

Remembering the night they spent together, Summer had to agree. He'd been ready all night long. Her face burned and she knew she'd turned red. What in the world had made her agree to meet him here?

As she exited the car, the dog, who lay panting at his feet, stood and wagged his stumpy tail.

"Who's this?" she asked, delighted at his friendliness.

"Boomer, meet Summer."

The animal trotted over. Still grasping the leash, Tony followed. Boomer sat down and lifted his paw.

"He wants to shake hands," Tony said.

Charmed, she complied. "Hi, Boomer. You're a sweetheart."

She swore the dog smiled. Then he plopped back onto the ground.

"By the looks of things, you two are having quite a workout," she said.

Tony lifted one broad shoulder. "A couple miles. You're all dressed up. That toe must be better—you're wearing heels and I don't see any sign of a limp."

"It's much better, thanks. I'm on the way home from a meeting at a temp agency."

"You've been laid off, what—almost a week? You don't waste any time."

"I can't afford to be unemployed. Boomer looks thirsty."

"We both are. We do this all the time. There's a drive-thru coffee place nearby, where we usually stop for water and a rest before we turn around and run home."

"I know that place. I used to get my coffee there on my way to work every morning. My house is closer."

OMG, had she just invited Tony over? Only because he and his dog needed water, she assured herself.

His eyes lit up and he flashed a grin. "Sounds good."

"Hop in."

He glanced down at himself. "Better not. I'm awful sweaty."

He certainly was. The wet patches darkening his shirt highlighted his considerable abs and flat belly. Summer swallowed. "I don't mind."

Understatement of the month.

Tony pulled his shirt over his head and wadded it up. "Open the trunk and I'll toss this in."

Who was she to argue? She popped the thing open.

In no time, Boomer was seated in the back and Tony buckled in next to her. He slid the seat all the way back to accommodate his long legs.

Summer forced her gaze to the road. She wouldn't let herself look at his fit, muscled gorgeousness... Much, anyway.

With vivid clarity she recalled his feverish hands all over her and the electric pleasure of his body joining with hers. Desire flared up and she shifted in her seat.

No. This afternoon was about giving water to a thirsty man and his dog, period.

He gave her a sideways look. "You're awful quiet and fidgety."

He would notice. "It's this suit and the rush-hour traffic," she lied.

"Those clothes look good. What happened at the temp agency?"

Embarrassed about the job she'd accepted, she stalled. "You really want to know?"

"Yeah."

"We're almost at my house. I'll tell you when we get there."

8

Tony hadn't expected to see Summer again. Now he and Boomer were in her car, on the way to her place.

Her tight skirt had ridden halfway up her smooth thighs. She looked as hot as she had in her party dress the other night. Damn, she was fine. And maybe more interested in him than she let on. He intended to find out.

As if she'd read his thoughts and sensed his hunger, she frowned and tugged the hem down with one hand.

Tony cleared his throat and noted the well-kept bungalows all around. "Nice area."

"I like it." She signaled and turned onto a two-lane road. "This is my street."

"I've been here before."

"Don't tell me one of the houses had a fire? That must've happened before I moved into the neighborhood."

For a few seconds, he debated what to say. But he had nothing to hide. "I once dated a woman up the block from here."

"No way. Let me guess—Selena Birch."

"How'd you know?"

"My other neighbors are either married or old enough to be your mother. Unless you prefer older women."

"I don't mind a woman a few years older than me, but fifty-seven?"

She laughed, a tinkling sound that filled the air. "What's so funny?" he asked, grinning along.

"The expression on your face. You looked like you swallowed a dead bug. So you and Selena dated."

"Not for long." Tony had tired of her. No chemistry.

Summer nodded. "Neither of you is the settling-down kind. We're here."

She turned up the short, gravel drive of a one-story tan rambler with dark brown trim. Under the living room window, a flower box with nothing in it but dirt.

"Cute place," he said as she pulled to a stop.

"It's small and the yard needs work, but it's mine. Or will be, eventually."

She looked nervous about that. Likely she was stressed about paying the mortgage now that she'd lost her job. A good reminder that she might need more from him than he could give.

"You're right, I'm not interested in settling down," he said, in case she'd forgotten. "Neither are you."

"Not for a long, long time."

This was good—if she truly meant it. With women, a guy never knew. They exited the car and headed across the yard.

"If you like to garden, you can do most of the yard work yourself," he said.

"I never tried till I bought the house the year before last. As you can see, I'm not great at it."

"When I bought my place and started the tree business, I wasn't, either."

"How did you learn?"

"Books, online, trial and error, talking with experts at nurseries and garden stores. I enjoy taking care of my yard."

"I never pegged you for a gardener. Hey, how are your trees?"

"Thriving. They like this warmer weather. Another week or two and they'll be ready for delivery."

"You have to dig them up?"

He shook his head. "I grow them in pots. Makes transporting them easy."

"I wondered. What happens when a tree outgrows its container?"

"I don't keep them long enough for that."

As she unlocked the front door, Tony bent down and took off his sneakers and socks. He left them beside the welcome mat.

"Thanks for removing your shoes. I don't wear mine inside, either. The floors stay a lot cleaner."

"Exactly. Grab me a rag and I'll wipe Boomer's paws."

She waved that away. "He's fine."

Inside, she stepped out of her heels and sighed. "Much better."

She placed the shoes and her purse on top of an antique trunk against the wall in the small, tidy area off the entry. A neat freak, like him. Another trait they shared.

What else did they have in common? Suddenly, he wanted to know everything about her.

She turned toward the hallway. "This way to the kitchen."

Once there, she gestured him to a table for four

that looked expensive, all gleaming wood and uphol-
stered chairs.

He hesitated. "I need to clean up before I sit on one
of those pretty chairs."

"Of course. The bathroom is on the other side of
the living room. There are towels in the linen closet.
While you're gone, I'll get Boomer something to
drink."

The feminine bathroom, painted a rosy apricot,
had gauzy, white curtains and white privacy shades. A
clear glass-enclosed shower contained a long-handled
back scrubber, hair products, and a pink razor.

Standing at the spotless white sink, he washed his
face, hair, and torso, then dried off with a fluffy towel
the color of green apples.

Curious, he peeked into the rooms at that end of
the house. Across the hall from the bathroom, a modest, uncluttered room with a desk, computer, and
bookshelf faced the back yard. Her bedroom was adjacent to the office. Whimsical framed pictures of doe-
eyed cats, brightly colored birds, and galloping mus-
tangs decorated the walls.

Sunbeams slanted across the queen-size bed. The
perfectly smooth spread matched the drapes, with a
handful of pastel throw pillows arranged against the
headboard.

Everything as tidy and subdued as the rest of the
house, as Summer herself.

Or so she seemed. Tony knew better. The cool, orderly façade concealed a passionate woman, uninhibited and unbridled in bed. He wanted to unleash that
fire again and bury himself in her soft heat.

That depended on her.

～

BOOMER HAD FINISHED LAPPING up his second bowl of water when Tony reentered the kitchen. His close-cropped dark hair was damp. He looked clean. Shirtless, barefoot, clad only in a pair of gym shorts, he also looked sexy.

Pretending she wasn't drooling, Summer pulled a glass from the cabinet. "Water or lemonade?"

"Water first, then lemonade."

She nodded and watched him fill his glass. "Would you like ice?"

"Straight from the tap is fine." Standing at the sink, he tilted his head back. Within seconds, he drained the glass.

Even watching his throat work was sheer pleasure and a welcome diversion from her troubles.

He wiped his mouth with the back of his hand, brought the empty glass to the table, and sat down. "Now I'm ready for that lemonade."

Summer retrieved the pitcher from the fridge. When she turned around, he was staring at her. "Is there something on the back of my skirt?" she asked.

His eyes flashed with heat. "You have great legs."

Nothing she hadn't heard before. Yet when Tony uttered the words, they seemed more genuine. Which was ridiculous. Tony was a red-blooded male. He looked, he liked, and he said so, and she wasn't naive enough to fall for this or any other line.

Still, she went all soft inside.

Be careful. She joined him at the kitchen table and poured the lemonade.

Boomer stretched out on the throw in front of the back door and made himself at home.

Determined not to think about sex, she steered the conversation to business. "How do you know when to deliver your trees to the nursery?"

"I contract with four different companies, and each has its own timeline. Although in the spring, they all expect their orders before Mother's Day."

"Four? You're more enterprising than I thought."

His eyes grew hooded. "Am I."

Summer did her best to explain. "The other night you downplayed the time you spend on your tree business, and I assumed..."

"That I'm not serious about it? Growing trees isn't half as intense as fighting fires, but nurturing them and keeping them healthy takes some effort." He squinted at her. "You keep unfolding and refolding that napkin. You did the same thing with your cocktail napkin the night of the wedding. You want those corners lined up."

Surprised he'd noticed, she set her glass on the napkin. "And you want people to think you're laid back when you're not. I'm a neat freak. What's your excuse?"

"Since you asked... When my mom got sick, I got scared. I didn't want her to worry about me, so I pretended to be calm and laid back. After a while, it became second nature."

"Interesting." Summer rarely talked about her childhood, but now that Tony had talked about his, she felt comfortable sharing. "I'm the opposite. Shelley wasn't sick, but she was unpredictable. Rainy and I never knew what to expect. Our mother's mood and our lives changed depending on whether she had a boyfriend, and whether or not they got along."

"That doesn't sound fun."

"It was chaotic, and there were times we didn't feel safe. All I wanted was stability, and I made up my mind to get it. I took charge of my life and my future, and gave my all to get ahead. I mapped out my life, and the strategy worked, at least job wise. On a personal level, things didn't work out so well."

"You mean your ex."

"Yes. My father, the boyfriends of my mom who treated me well, guys I dated—every one of them left. I saved my heart for the one man I believed would stick around. I thought Lee and I were so well matched, and in some areas, we were. But not where it counted. My heart was in tatters, but at least I had the job of my dreams—until last Friday." She realigned her glass so that it sat exactly in the center of the napkin. "Right now, I'd settle for a basic accounting job."

Tony nodded. "Smart of you to sign on with a temp agency."

"They found me a job at an accounting firm, only not as an accountant." Summer explained about the woman she was subbing for.

"I don't see you as a receptionist."

"Hey, it's a paycheck. Who knows, when the company has an opening in accounting, maybe they'll think of me."

"You never know. The other night you mentioned severance pay. Why not use it and hold out for the job you want?"

"Two months' salary won't last long. Believe me, I'm doing everything I can think of to find a position." Summer didn't want to talk about herself anymore. Too depressing. "Tell me about your work this week."

"We had a car fire, a freak accident where a man tipped over a crane he was speed-driving, and a nasty warehouse fire. During the night, there were a couple of medical issues and accidents. This year, Nate and I are in charge of the annual fundraiser and community barbecue, and between calls we worked on the details."

"When is that?"

"The first Saturday in June. That's about a month from now, so there's a lot to do."

"You're busy."

"Always. I heard from my mom. She said you called today."

"Her and a lot of other clients. Any day now, TME will send out a notice about my leaving, and I want to contact them all before the letters go out."

"I told her we saw each other at the wedding. Now she thinks something's going on with us."

"Oh?"

"Yep." His long, steamy look set off all kinds of crazy inside. Summer's entire body perked up. She rolled the cool glass between her hands. "Has she scheduled a doctor's appointment?"

"This Friday."

"You'll let me know what happens?"

"As soon as I have something to share. About you and me—I don't think what I'm feeling is one-sided."

Another smoldering look and she almost went up in flames. "What exactly are you feeling?" she asked, stalling for time.

"If I'd shaved before I went out running and didn't stink, I'd show you."

"Beards don't bother me." She sniffed. "All I smell is the lavender soap from the bathroom."

His mouth quirked. "Just what I wanted, to smell like a girl. Way to kill the mood."

If anything, his humor only added to her attraction. Forget being careful. She was in big trouble, and by his cocky expression he knew it.

Before she could blink he was at her side, pulling her to her feet. She didn't stop him.

9

Summer's lowered eyelids almost hid the heat in her eyes. A clear message that regardless what she said, she still wanted Tony as bad as he wanted her. He grasped her shoulders and brushed his lips over hers, teasing and testing.

Her response was instant and eager, and he pulled back to smile. "I'm right—you feel this connection, too."

He fused his mouth to hers, tasting lemonade, woman, and a hunger as fierce as his own.

Clutching his shoulders, she pressed in tight, her soft curves fitting his hard places. Hungry and growling, he palmed her soft butt and brought her closer. As close as two people could get in clothes.

He slid his hands under her skirt and up the smooth backs of her thighs. All the way up to her panties and under the elastic.

Her low moan throbbed through him. He wanted to drag her down to the kitchen floor and bury himself in her welcoming heat. He nuzzled the crook of her neck. "God, I want you."

He started to unbutton her blouse. She batted him away. "We have to stop."

Confused, he held up both hands and stepped back. "You don't kiss me like you want to stop."

She wouldn't meet his eyes. "I can't get involved with you."

He laughed softly. "Sweetheart, you already are."

"Well, I don't want to be."

"What you don't want is to fall in love. Neither do I. Like I said before, we don't have to get serious to enjoy each other. We proved that the night of the wedding."

A look of pure longing crossed her face before she folded her arms over the breasts he coveted.

"Look, I know your ex did a number on you, but I'm not like him," he said. "When I'm with someone, I'm *with* them for as long as it lasts. I don't cheat. No one else knows this, but you're the first woman I've been with in months. You're the one I want."

The only one. He had no idea why, but there it was.

"You could have any female in town," she said. "Why me?"

"I..." He broke off. "Don't make me tell you."

"Now you have to."

They returned to the table and sat down.

"At first, I gravitated toward you because you know my mother and I was—am—freaked about her health. You were different than I imagined. You ate without worrying about your weight and you danced like a wild woman, not at all the prim and proper accountant I assumed you were. You have a great body and beautiful legs, and when you planted that hot kiss on me in the bathroom that night... Not even a eunuch could resist that."

She looked embarrassed. "Because I overdid the champagne."

"Which led to a night I won't soon forget. You're

jeans and a top, and transferred his shirt to the dryer. Then she fixed herself dinner.

By the time she finished eating and tidied up the kitchen, Tony's tee was clean and dry. For reasons she couldn't explain, instead of folding it she buried her nose in the worn cotton. Detergent had washed away any scent of him, but not the memory of his mouth and hands on her...

Burning for him all over again, she left the shirt on the dryer and returned to the kitchen. Standing at the counter, she opened her laptop and checked for available accounting jobs. Nothing new.

She wandered back to the laundry area and exchanged her top for Tony's tee. The thing swam on her, the sleeves nearly to her elbows and the hem halfway down her thighs.

Comfy and soft, it made her feel warm inside. If she closed her eyes she could almost imagine him holding her. Sinking against the dryer, she let out a sigh of pleasure. And admitted that she agreed with him. As Dorie had pointed out, they'd already had sex several times—heck, they'd spent an entire night together. Holding back now made no sense, especially when neither of them wanted a real relationship.

Maybe a physical relationship wasn't such a bad idea.

Summer's body cheered at that, but she wasn't going to give in just yet. Instead of letting her desire guide her, she would make this decision her usual, rational way. Armed with a pen and paper, she headed for her office and plunked down at the desk. There she made a list.

PROS:

about the sexiest woman I've ever known, and
being deep inside you. I think about it all the time

Something soft and warm flickered in her
Then she blinked and her chin jutted up. "I
enough on my mind right now. I don't need you
plicating my life even more."

Nope, she wasn't into depending on him, not
for sex.

"Suit yourself." He brushed his thumb over
bottom lip. Her eyes went hazy and he let out a
laugh. "If you change your mind, you know wher
find me. Thanks for the water break."

He whistled for Boomer, leashed him, and ope
the door. "Come on, buddy, let's go home."

~

NOT LONG AFTER Tony and his dog left, Sum
realized he'd forgotten his T-shirt. She pictured
running across the meadow bare-chested. E
woman with eyes would salivate.

She wasn't about to contact him about the tee.
didn't want him to come back right now, not when
was still on fire. Putting a stop to the pleasure h
been easy. She'd told him no, but her desire for
had almost won out.

Now his sweat-soaked shirt lay in her trunk
couldn't leave it there to mildew. Once she was
side, she ran her hand over the trunk. Was it wa
to the touch than usual, or was she overheated?

Regardless, the shirt needed to come out
popped the latch, reached inside, and snatche
sweaty thing between two fingers. Holding it at
length, she brought it inside and dropped i
washer. She hung up her work outfit, change

1. Tony provides a welcome distraction from worries.

CONS:

1. Distraction interferes with focus on the job search.

2. Getting involved solely for physical reasons poses the risk of becoming too emotionally involved.

3. Tony's reputation almost guarantees a bad ending and further disruption from the job search.

FINISHED, she set down the pen. And look at that—the cons won by a two-point margin. She'd been right to call a halt to tonight, yet she didn't feel as self-righteous as she should have.

Wearing Tony's T-shirt wasn't helping. Returning to the laundry area, she changed back into her own top. She folded the tee and left it on the dryer.

Too antsy to sit, she bounced from room to room, closing the drapes and flipping on lights.

There. Now what?

She needed to get out of here. Cookies, she wanted cookies, the chocolate, chewy kind. Time for a run to the store. Keys and purse in hand, she stepped onto the porch.

The sun had set and the air had cooled. Summer rubbed her arms. And there was Tony's ex, Selena, sauntering toward her. Curvy, with short, dyed red hair, she filled out her low-cut top and jeans in a way Summer never could.

More acquaintances than friends, they mainly spoke when they bumped into each other in the neighborhood.

"Hi," Summer said, using a smile to mask her restlessness. "Haven't seen you in ages."

"You wouldn't believe the number of students applying to the college for summer quarter." Selena worked in marketing and admissions at the Guff's Lake branch of Rogue Valley Community College. "How's work for you?"

Summer filled her in on the changes in her life. "I'm looking for a new job."

"With your degree and experience, you're bound to find something. Did I see Tony Clark leave your house a little while ago—without a shirt?" Selena fanned herself. "I had no idea you knew him."

"I do his mom's taxes—or did, before I was laid off. That's how we met."

"Now he's coming over to see you? You two must've hit it off real well."

More than Selena would ever know. "It's not what you think. When I drove home from the temp agency this afternoon, I saw him and his dog running through a field along the road. They were tired and thirsty and I invited them to stop here for water."

"Way to get the guy into your house." Selena licked her lips. "I'll have to remember that one."

"You don't need any tricks—men fall all over you."

Her neighbor smiled. "Some of them. What happened to Tony's shirt?"

"It was drenched with sweat from his running and he didn't want to get my furniture dirty. So he took it off. Then when he left, he forgot it."

"I'd take dirty with Tony any time." Selena licked her lips. "He sure knows his way around a kiss."

Among other things. Summer imagined him and her neighbor in bed together and fought a scowl. "He mentioned that you'd dated," she said, casual as you please.

"Did he. That was a good three years ago and we only went out twice. We never did more than kiss, and not much of that, but not for lack of trying on my part. He wasn't interested."

Two dates and no sex? Summer felt much better.

"I really liked him, but he didn't feel the same about me," Selena said. "Now you're dating him. I'm jealous."

Summer shook her head. "We're..." What exactly were they? *Friends* wasn't quite right, and *lovers for one night, possibly more if I'm willing* didn't work, either. "I've never gone out with him," she said. Technically, if you didn't count dancing and talking for hours, then spending a whole night in each other's arms.

"I'd bet my new bikini he'll ask you out. Be careful —after a few dates he'll move on to someone else."

Not exactly a news flash. "Thanks for the warning." Summer checked her watch. "I need to get to the store before it closes."

She bought enough ice cream sandwiches and cookies to last the week, along with other essentials. Before leaving the store, she opened a package of pinwheels, and by the time she pulled back into her driveway, she'd eaten half of them.

Not that the sugar did a thing to lift her spirits. For that, she needed a job. Feeling dismal, she put the rest of the groceries away.

"Things will look better after a good night's sleep," she told herself.

In the laundry room, she tugged off her clothes and put them in the dirty laundry basket.

Tony's shirt lay on the dryer where she'd left it. She ran her fingers over the faded logo. Driven by a compulsion she didn't understand, she stripped off her bra and panties, then pulled the tee over her head.

As she padded to the bedroom, the soft cotton brushed her thighs and caressed her breasts. Her lonely nipples stood at attention.

In bed, she closed her eyes and imagined Tony's hands on her everywhere. Moaning, she shifted restlessly and got wet between her legs. "At this rate, I'll never get to sleep," she muttered.

And yet she settled right down. Her last thoughts before falling into dreamland were of him.

10

Tony and his mom sat in the oncologist's waiting room along with other patients, some painfully thin and others appearing to be healthy, but all as somber and preoccupied as he was.

He had no idea whether today's appointment was a false alarm or a real concern. His mother shifted in her seat, rifled through her purse, crossed one leg and then the other, reminding him of when she'd had breast cancer.

"You're working yourself up, Ma. Take a few deep breaths."

She nodded and complied, then reached for his hand. "You're my rock, my beacon of strength. You always have been."

Okay, now he was seriously freaked out, and right back there when he'd been sixteen. Scared and feeling powerless to help her. He gave her hand a reassuring squeeze. "You'll be fine, Ma. I'm not worried."

Pure bull. Thanks to the calm, I'm good expression he'd perfected all those years ago, she had no idea how spooked he was.

A nurse he recognized from years ago, now in her

fifties, entered the waiting room, clipboard and files in hand. "Irene Clark," she called out.

Tony and his mom stood.

The nurse smiled at them. "Hi, Irene. Tony, I haven't seen you since you were in high school—except, of course, on the calendar. You're a superstar."

He didn't feel like one. "Hey, Bonita. Are you taking youth pills? 'Cause you look ten years younger than you did last time I saw you."

"Aren't you sweet? I lost fifty pounds."

"How on earth did you do it?" Tony's mom, always fighting excess weight, asked.

"I gave up sugary colas and started walking every day."

"I don't drink cola, but maybe I'll try walking," Tony's mom said. "If I'm not sick," she added under her breath.

"Do you want me in the exam room with you?" he asked.

"Please."

In the little room, Bonita gestured him to use the empty chair while she weighed his mother and measured her height. Next, she perched on the exam table and Bonita checked her temperature, blood pressure, and pulse.

"Dr. Geddes will be in shortly," she said.

Moments later, his mother's oncologist from all those years ago entered the room. Silver-haired, with a calm manner and a gentle, yet commanding voice, she greeted his mother warmly.

"Good to see you again, Irene. I saw you a few months ago for your annual checkup. What seems to be the problem today?"

His mother heaved a fear-laced breath. "I found

lumps in my breast and I'm bloated and uncomfortable."

Dr. Geddes nodded and began asking questions, typing into her laptop as his mother talked. Tony learned a lot. He hadn't thought to ask about her symptoms.

He stepped out while the doctor examined her breasts and otherwise examined her. When the woman summoned him in again, he returned to his chair.

"I don't hear anything that alarms me," she said. "You don't have a fever and your vital signs are normal, but those lumps are a concern. They could be cysts, but we need to find out. I'm going to order new blood work, X-rays, and several tests. Stop at the front desk on your way out and get on the schedule."

"Then what?" Tony asked.

"Once the tests are done and results come in, I'll call your mother."

They left with the clinic with the tests scheduled for the following week.

"After talking to Dr. Geddes, I feel better," his mother said on the way out.

Tony didn't, not with those lumps she'd reported. "You're in good hands, that's for sure. Hey, do you want to have lunch at The Rogue?"

"If we're quick. I need to get to the store."

If she wanted to work, she must not feel that bad.

At first his mother picked at her food, but in the end, she ate a fair amount. When he dropped her off later, she seemed like her normal self.

False alarm, he thought. Prayed.

He considered phoning Summer to let her know about the appointment, but she'd insisted she didn't want to get involved with him, and like it or not, he meant to respect that. Best wait till he had something definitive to tell her.

~

THE SUN WAS STARTING to rise when Summer drove to Rosemary's Breakfast Nook for the 6:30 a.m. women's networking breakfast meeting. The early start enabled people to get to work by 8:00. And a good thing, as the receptionist Summer was filling in for had been selected as a jury member. What had been a two-day temp job had been extended until the trial ended.

Earning money, even a paltry amount, was good, but after almost a week of answering phones, which didn't ring often now that Tax Day was over, she was losing her mind. Reading a novel and checking for jobs online helped pass the hours, but she still had far too much time to brood.

She'd planned carefully for this meeting and intended to put the word out that she was looking for a new job. Which was why she'd stocked her briefcase-size purse with résumés and newly printed personal business cards.

The instant she entered the restaurant, delicious smells tempted her. Strong coffee, buttery eggs and bacon, fresh-baked Samantha's Treats, and other delectables... Her stomach gurgled in anticipation.

The place was packed, and as always, the staff had pushed several tables together to accommodate the twelve to fifteen women who showed up at the monthly breakfasts.

"It's good to see you, Summer," Lana Jackman greeted her. Wiry and about Summer's age, she was the organization's president. "It's been months."

"You know how busy things are during tax season."

"Ugh, don't mention the 'T' word. This year, I had to drain my savings to pay what I owe."

Despite Lana's lament, she wore a smile. It was no secret that keeping her furniture rental company afloat had been a struggle.

"Business must be picking up," Summer said.

"Finally. After almost three years, we're solidly in the black. Thanks in part to our hot real estate and housing market. Houses sell faster when they're staged with quality furnishings, and renting furnished apartments are the current rage around here. You look great—healthy and rested. What's your secret?"

For all Summer's worries, she'd been sleeping well. She credited Tony's T-shirt for that. For some reason, when she wore it to bed she slept like a baby. She wanted to keep it forever.

Who knew, that could happen by default. She hadn't heard from him since he'd left it in the trunk. He didn't seem to care, but then, with something that faded and old, who would?

She supposed she ought to be grateful he'd stayed away. Heck, she'd told him to. Yet she thought constantly about him. But not today. "My company downsized and let a bunch of us go," she said. "I'm looking for a new job."

Lana's eyebrows shot up. "I'm sorry. And glad you're here."

"Me, too. If you come across an opening for a seasoned accountant... Let me give you my résumé and a card with my contact info." Summer slid the items from her purse and handed them to the woman.

"I'll keep my eyes and ears open." Lana scanned the résumé. "You know what... Jolynn Glick and Renee Paley are here. You should talk to them." She nodded at the far end of the table, where the two forty-some-thing women stood chatting quietly.

Both had worked at reputable CPA firms before they left to start their own partnership the previous year. Summer had no interest in going out on her own, but maybe they knew of an opening that hadn't been posted. "Thanks, I will," she said.

The two women were about to sit down. Hoping to join them, she hurried over. "I'm looking for a new job," she said after they exchanged greetings. "Lana suggested you might know of something."

Jolynn and Renee shared a look.

"It just so happens, we do," Jolynn said. Both women gave Summer their cards.

"Paley and Glick," Summer read on both. "Nice cards. I'm in awe at what you've done." And a little scared even thinking about it. "Going out on your own —that's a gutsy move."

"Not if you're ready. We tossed the idea around for years. Imagine a female-owned and operated ac-counting firm."

Rare and exciting. "I love the idea," Summer said.

Renee smiled. "We're looking for a senior manager with an eye toward making partner within the next five years. Are you interested?"

Well, yeah. "Very much. I'd like to know more."

"So would we."

Once again, Summer dipped into her purse for her résumé and card.

Jolynn gestured at the empty chairs in front of them. "Sit with us and we'll talk."

Over breakfast, Summer learned more about the company.

"We had a strong first year, exceeding our projections," Jolynn said, sharing percentages and other details.

Renee nodded. "Next year, we expect to double those numbers. We're looking for someone with strong management and marketing skills."

Summer had both. "The accountants I managed and my admin assistant will vouch for my management skills. As for marketing, last year I brought in more new business than anyone else. My former boss, Malcolm Tillinger, will give you a recommendation." She'd call him today. "You should also know that I signed a non-solicitation clause that stays in effect for a year," she added.

"Didn't we all," Renee said. "If your marketing skills are as good as you say, that won't be a problem. We'll look for that recommendation."

Summer liked everything she heard although given a choice, she preferred a stable firm with a strong track record. Then again, TME had had an excellent track record and look how that'd turned out.

But if Paley and Glick thrived...

Not so fast. This is simply a conversation.

Still, she couldn't help but be excited. As hope struggled with common sense—no point getting worked up just yet—Summer stopped at the bathroom. When she returned to the dining area, everyone from the meeting had left and the tables had been bussed, cleaned, and reset for another large group.

She bought herself a Samantha's blueberry muffin for later. As she opened the door to leave, a group of striking men ambled across the parking lot toward the entrance. She recognized them from the calendar and the wedding. Firefighters, and Tony was with them.

They were all big, muscular, and sinfully good-looking, but he stood out. Confident and in earnest

conversation with several of the men, he took her
breath away.

She was glued to the threshold, staring with her
tongue practically hanging out when he spotted her.
His face lit in a grin that made her knees tremble, and
he made a beeline for her.

11

After a brutal two days that kept Tony on his toes 24/7, he looked forward to a hearty breakfast followed by a few hours' sleep. One look at Summer and he forgot his fatigue. Wearing a silky, feminine blouse, a snug-fitting skirt, and fairly high heels, her hair sleek and smooth, she looked a lot like she had the day he'd met her—professional, cool, and aloof.

He knew better, had made her shiver and moan. Was she wearing a lacy bra and a thong underneath these work clothes?

Down, boy. "Never figured I'd run into you here on a Wednesday morning," he said.

"This is where my professional women's networking group meets for breakfast once a month."

"No kidding. My crewmates and I come here most Wednesdays after we clock out. Strange that we didn't see each other till this morning."

"My group is usually gone by 7:45. Today I stayed behind to chat with two of the women."

Fortunately for him. "You look very professional." And hot.

"That's what I aimed for. I came to network. I have to be at work in thirty minutes."

"Still temping, huh?"

She rolled her eyes. "Unfortunately. I'm so ready for a real job."

Gus and Nate joined them. "Hey," Gus said. "Last time I saw you, you were barefoot and heading for your car in the hotel garage."

Her cheeks flushed a pretty pink.

"You look good," Nate said.

"Thanks. I had a meeting."

Feeling possessive, Tony cupped her elbow. "Why don't you stick around for a while and join us?"

Gus nodded. "Wanda should be here any minute. I know she'd like to see you."

Adam sauntered over and added, "Sam, too."

"You're back from your honeymoon," Summer said. "You're all tan and rested."

"Acapulco is a great place to relax. Sam should be here in a few minutes."

"I'd like to see both her and Wanda, but I already ate and I have to be somewhere. I was laid off from my accounting job, and I'm heading to my temp job. Tell Sam I'll call this afternoon and explain."

Adam nodded. "Will do. Bummer."

"We hadn't heard." Nate jerked his thumb Tony's way. "That one there didn't tell us."

"I asked him not to." She smiled at Tony, and he figured he'd earned a few brownie points for keeping his word. "It's not a secret anymore. If you hear of anything..."

Not ready to let her go, Tony held onto her. "I'm going to walk Summer to her car," he announced. "Nate, order me a four-egg cheese omelet, sausage, and two scones."

Summer's eyes widened. "That's a lot of food."

"We had a busy night and I haven't eaten since dinner."

"Define 'busy.'"

"Between twenty-three hundred hours and five a.m., we fought two fires and made two rescue calls. Each time we had to clean and restock the vehicles and file reports."

"That's busy, all right. No wonder you ordered so much breakfast."

"You forget, I've seen you put away quite a bit of food yourself."

"Not as often as you think. I'll bet you never gain weight."

"Nope, and neither do you."

"Not usually, but lately... I haven't worn this skirt in months and it's a little snug around the waist. I've been doing a lot of stress eating."

"You look good to me." He let his gaze travel from her head to her sexy heels, gratified when her lips parted as if begging him to run his thumb over the bottom one. He was tempted to do it, but held off. "I left my T-shirt in the trunk of your car. When can I pick it up?"

"Anytime. Speaking of your shirt, after you left last week, Selena stopped by. I think she wants to date you again."

"She's not for me. What I said before holds— you're the woman I want." Summer held his gaze long enough to fire him up, big time.

"I didn't think you cared about that old shirt," she said.

"The opposite. Five years ago I bought it to celebrate my five-year anniversary at the station. It's one of my favorites."

"Then why haven't you called or stopped by to pick it up?"

"I didn't want to crowd you. You haven't called me, either."

"Crowd me?"

"You said you didn't want to see me. Plus, being alone with you is dangerous."

She didn't argue with that. In the morning sunlight, her eyes were the color of dark honey. Inviting and warm. "I'll drop it by the station."

"Nah. If you meant what you said about stopping by, I'll do that sometime this week. So you don't like the temp job."

"Answering phones weeks after the end of the tax season is a total bore. Most of the accountants and staff are away on vacation."

"A waste of your talent. Did you get any good leads at the breakfast?" he said as they neared her car.

"A really good one. Last year, Jolynn and Renee, the two women I mentioned talking with, started their own CPA firm. They're looking for a senior manager— the same position I applied for when TME laid me off. They asked for my résumé."

"Way to go."

She hesitated. "Cross your fingers."

"You're not sure about this company," he guessed.

"How did you know?"

"You pushed your hair behind your ears twice when it's already tucked back there."

"Do you always notice details like that?"

"When I'm interested in someone."

She started to do it again, but caught herself. "The business is fairly new, and working there poses certain risks. If it fails, I'm out of a job again. But if it thrives, I can make partner in five years."

"Which is exactly what you want."

Her jaw dropped. "How do you do that?"

"Do what?"

"Cut straight to the bottom line. My dream has always been to make partner."

"You mentioned that at the after-party. There you are. Go out and get that job."

"Yes, sir! First, they have to want me. They might, but we need to talk more."

"As wary as you say you are, by the sparkle in your eyes and the color in your cheeks, you're also happy about this."

"After three weeks of 'No thank you,' it's nice to have a solid nibble."

Her smile dazzled him. She looked radiant. Damn, he wanted to kiss her. So he did.

She didn't fight him, her mouth as sweet and welcoming as ever. He was getting into it when she placed both palms on his chest and shoved him away.

"People can see us!" she said, shooting him a dirty look.

Unrepentant, he shrugged. "Couldn't help myself. Your high spirits are contagious. I'm pulling for you."

"Thanks. How was your mother's doctor appointment?"

Way to douse his good mood. He sobered. "The doctor found lumps in her breasts. My mom is having blood tests and a breast imaging exam today. Tomorrow, she gets a colonoscopy and an endoscopy to check her intestines and digestive system."

"Sounds thorough but also nerve-wracking. Are you worried?"

"Yeah, but I'm putting on a brave front. She's uptight enough without me adding to it."

Summer nodded. "Calm and laid-back, like when

you were in high school." She glanced at her watch. "You probably want to join your friends and I have to get to that receptionist job."

She headed for her car with a bounce in her step and a seductive sway to her hips. Looking over her shoulder, she waved.

And Tony knew they weren't through, not by a long shot.

~

As DULL AS playing receptionist for a mostly empty office was, finding out the end was in sight plunged Summer's flagging morale into a dismal tailspin. Not counting today, she had three days left on the job— tomorrow, Monday, and Tuesday. Either she needed to secure more temporary work or find a permanent job, and fast. Meanwhile, she'd better apply for unemployment.

Nothing she could do about any of those tonight. Determined to chill out for the evening, she changed into Tony's T-shirt and her robe, then plopped in front of the TV with a container of leftover Chinese takeout.

When that was gone, she padded into the kitchen to grab a package of oatmeal chocolate chip cookies. Just then, the doorbell rang.

And here she was, dressed for bed. She peered through a chink in the drapes to see who was at her door and saw Tony and Boomer, his stumpy tail wagging.

No doubt they'd come to pick up the shirt she happened to be wearing. God only knew what he'd think about that. After pulling her robe together and tightening the sash, she opened the door. With a happy woof, Boomer raced at her. She laughed and instantly felt better. "I'm glad to see you, too."

Tony took in her robe and bare feet. "You okay?"

"It's been a stressful day. I'm relaxing."

"Stressed because?"

"My job ends Tuesday and I don't have anything else lined up." She eyed the two double-scoop ice cream cones in the cardboard carrier he held. "Is one of those for me?"

"Yep. Take your pick—peanut butter and chocolate or caramel swirl and rocky road."

Her mouth watered. "I think I love you. Peanut butter and chocolate, please."

His lips quirked. "You don't really love me."

"No, but I'm crazy about ice cream—especially chocolate."

"Just call me your stress buster."

Tony lifted the cones out of the holder. The scoops in both had started to melt, and she licked hers all the way around, neatly catching the drips.

His eyelids heavy, Tony did the same with his cone. Between his smoldering eyes and his tongue thoroughly laving the globes of ice cream, she almost combusted.

"It's a nice evening and I don't mind standing on the front porch with you," he drawled, "but now that we've cleaned these things up, I'd rather be inside."

The house or her body? Tearing her gaze from his, she opened the door a little wider to let him enter. "Did I miss something yesterday at Rosemary's? Was I supposed to know you'd be here tonight?"

He toed out of his shoes and left them beside the welcome mat. "I said I'd stop by sometime this week to pick up my T-shirt. Here I am."

Uh-oh. "If I'd known, I'd have washed it."

"I don't expect you to do that. Unless you left it in the trunk of your car. In that case, it's probably a lost cause. I shouldn't have waited so long."

Summer shook her head. "Your tee is fine. I laundered it a few hours after you left that day. "

He looked relieved. "Then you don't need to wash it again."

"Yes, I do."

He frowned. "I'm not following."

Nothing to do but explain. "I've kinda sorta been sleeping in it."

"You sleep in my old shirt." He shook his head. "Why?"

Feeling sheepish, she studied her cone. "I don't know what made me put it on the first time, except that the fabric is worn and extra soft. With the stress of losing my job, I needed soft. I hadn't been sleeping well, but for some reason when I wear that shirt to bed, I sleep great."

"Seriously? The thing must be huge on you."

"And super comfy."

"Hey, if my tee helps you sleep... Keep it."

"But it's your favorite."

"I'll live. Besides, I like the idea of you in my shirt. You're wearing it now, right? Can I see?"

Taking her robe off was asking for trouble. "In the middle of our ice cream? I'd rather sit at the kitchen table and finish these things before we make a huge mess. Wish I had something for you, Boomer."

"He'll survive."

As if proving the point, the dog stretched out on the rug in front of the back door and took a nap.

"Have you thought any more about that accounting firm?" he asked.

"I sure have, especially now that my temp job is ending."

"What's the next step?"

"After work tomorrow, I'm going to drive past their offices to see what the building looks like and what kind of neighborhood they're in."

"Cool." Tony popped the last of his cone into his mouth. "Man, that was good." He stood. "Now I need to wash my hands."

He stood at the kitchen sink. With his back to Summer, she could study him freely. Such broad shoulders. A tight rear end and jeans that outlined his muscular legs. She craved him worse than chocolate.

"Any word on your mother's tests?" she asked as she joined him to rinse her own sticky fingers.

"We should have the results Monday."

In bare feet, she felt small beside him. He handed her the dish towel. She dried her hands and returned it to the towel bar.

"We both have a lot on our minds," she said.

"All I'm thinking about now is you in my shirt. Our ice cream is gone—time to take off that robe." She hesitated. "Come on, Summer. That tee is my fave and I gave it to you. The least you can do is let me see you in it."

He gave her a pleading, puppy-dog look no woman could resist. She sighed. "Oh, all right, but it's so big on me, it hides everything. Don't expect much."

She dropped her robe on the back of her chair, then pivoted around. The raw heat in his eyes made her feel naked and sexy. There went her body again, tingling and aware and wanting him.

This was dangerous.

"Why are you looking at me like that, when there's nothing to see?" She started to reach for her robe.

"Hey, I'm not through checking you out. That shirt never looked this good on me."

"With your chest and shoulders? I don't have many curves to begin with, and what little I have is totally covered."

"Not everything." He nodded at her breasts. "You're not wearing a bra. Hey, you got ice cream on yourself."

"With my robe closed tight?" She glanced down. "Where?"

"Not tight enough. Ice cream—right...there." He slid his finger slowly down the slope of her breast, stopping a hair's breadth above her areola.

Shamelessly begging for his attention, both nipples sharpened and ached.

"Can't have you sleeping in a dirty shirt."

He wet his fingers in the sink, then slowly rubbed the spot—and lower. Sucking in a breath, she gripped the counter behind her to keep her standing upright. "Tony, I..."

Immediately, he paused and lifted his arm. "You want me to stop, say the word."

She should, but... She returned his hand to her nipple and he went back to making her squirm. Delicious sensations spiraled from her breast to her stomach and further south. Her eyes drifted shut and she moaned.

He made a sound of pure masculine pleasure. "Turning you on is such a trip."

"You're good at it."

He pulled away and eyed her. "Got rid of the ice cream spot, but now you look like a lopsided wet T-shirt competition. Can't have one dry side, not with your compulsion for lining things up."

He repeated the whole addictive process on the

other nipple. Her knees wobbled and threatened to buckle. "I need to sit down," she said.

"Up you go." She was thin but no lightweight, yet Tony lifted her to the counter as if she weighed nothing.

He stepped in close between her thighs, tilted her chin up, and brushed his mouth over hers. Nibbling, coaxing, then settling in for long, deep kisses that burned through her.

Summer hooked her legs around his hips and brought the neediest part of her flush with his erection. He was hard, so hard.

Much better, but not close enough.

"Please," she whispered.

With the low laugh that vibrated through all her intimate parts, he slid the finger that had started all the thrumming inside her panties, straight to her sweet spot.

His turn to groan. "You're wet."

No arguing there. "Maybe I should take off my undies," she said, wriggling against his magic finger.

He was tugging them down when Boomer barked, scrambled to his feet, and raced to the back door. A knock followed.

"Summer, are you in there?"

Of all the times... "That's Selena," Summer hissed in Tony's ear, then caught the lobe in her teeth.

He swore softly. "Maybe she'll go away."

"With Boomer making all that noise? She knows we're in here." Summer raised her voice. "Be right there."

She slid to the floor, straightened her panties, and smoothed the tee over her hips. The wet spots Tony had made emphasized her rigid nipples. He retrieved her robe from the back of the chair and helped her into it.

After running a hand through her hair and tightening the sash, she unlocked the door.

12

An instant before Summer let Selena in, Tony grabbed the dish towel to cover himself—he was still hard—and pretended to dry his hands.

"Hi there," Summer said. She sounded normal, but the flush of arousal staining her cheeks gave her away.

"I saw Tony's car and thought I'd stop by and say hello," Selena said. "I hope I'm not intruding, although it looks as if I am."

She sure was. Tony and Summer were nowhere near finished. He wanted to make her lose control, wanted to be inside her.

"This must be the night to drop in," Summer said. "First Tony, now you. If I'd known, I'd be in day clothes instead of my robe."

"Hey, Selena." His body calmed, Tony hung up the towel.

"Hello there." She gave him a saucy look and her red lips formed a flirty smile. Her breasts almost swelled out of her top, but she wasn't Summer and left him cold.

"It's been a long time," Selena said. "How have you been?"

"Not bad. You?"

"Doing well. I didn't realize... Summer said you two weren't seeing each other."

"We're not," Summer stated.

"We are," Tony countered at the same time.

Selena glanced from one to the other. "Which is it?"

Tony put his arm around Summer's shoulders. "We definitely are."

Summer gave him a *Who says?* look. "We haven't discussed that. Can I get you a glass of lemonade, Selena?"

"As much as I'd love to be a fly on the wall while you two hash out whether or not you're involved, I wouldn't dream of staying. Good night."

Summer saw her out. On the back step, Selena lowered her voice and said something to her. Tony couldn't make out the words.

"Why did you tell Selena we're seeing each other?" Summer asked when she and Tony were alone again.

"Because it's true. We saw each other at Rosemary's and I'm with you tonight."

"We ran into each other at Rosemary's, and you stopped by here to pick up your shirt."

"Which you confiscated for yourself."

"I offered to give it back, and that has nothing to do with my question. Running into each other for all of ten minutes and your being here now is hardly 'seeing' each other."

She looked cute and cozy in her robe, but underneath she was wearing his shirt—braless and in bikini panties. She slept in the damn thing, which pleased him no end. Turned him on, too. "I disagree. If Selena hadn't interrupted, I'd be buried inside you right now."

The flush on her face deepened before she compressed her lips and set her hands on her hips. "Don't try to change the subject. We are not officially together."

"We could be." As soon as he said the words, he knew he wanted that. "What did Selena say about me when she left?"

"She reminded me that you're the love 'em and leave 'em kind. I've heard that before."

"Have you." He eyed her. "From who?"

"I don't remember. Does it matter?"

"Yeah—it makes me sound like a jerk." He crossed his arms. "I've always laid my cards on the table. Any woman I date knows exactly where I stand. I don't see that as a problem. Do you?"

"Well, no, but..."

"But what? You want me to leave you alone, say it." Hoping to hell she didn't, he sucked in a breath.

"Yes. No. I don't know. I'm all confused."

Her bare foot tapped silently on the tile floor. Even that turned him on.

"I haven't changed my mind, Summer. I think we should be together, right out in the open. I want people to know."

"You mean like a couple."

"For now."

"This whole conversation is making me nervous." She jammed her hands into the pockets of her robe.

She was more spooked about the couple thing than he was, which was reassuring. "The bottom line is the same as the last time we talked—you want me and I want you. Why torture ourselves?"

"Torture—clever. Does that line usually work?"

"I've never said it to anyone else—you're the one and only."

"Don't BS me, Tony."

"Swear to God. I wouldn't lie to you. Honesty is important to me."

Her believing him mattered, and he cupped her chin for some heavy eye contact. At last she nodded, and the tension in his gut eased.

"No pressure on either of us," he said. "We'll do this with open eyes and an agreement to keep the relationship light. When we stop having fun—"

"We go our separate ways."

"Exactly. You good with that?"

She hesitated, pushing her hair behind her ears and squinting as if in deep thought. "I think so. Now what?"

"We could both use a break from the stuff that's weighing on us. For you, what to decide about the accounting company you're visiting tomorrow, and what to do if they offer you a job. They will. For me, my mom's health. I won't know what results of her tests will show till Monday.

"I have a busy couple of days, delivering my trees to the nurseries and finalizing details for the fundraiser and barbecue, but I need more than work to get me through the weekend. Let's do something fun. Are you free Saturday?"

"I have plans with Dorie and Rainy in the morning, but the afternoon is wide open. What do you have in mind?"

Tony could think of a lot of things, most of them involving getting naked. But that could wait. "How about a game of mini-golf. Then I'll make you dinner."

"You're going to cook." She looked skeptical.

He laughed. "I'm no Guy Fieri, but I do all right. Especially when we're talking barbecue. Nobody grills steaks like me. The secret is in the sauce, and mine is dynamite."

"You're making my mouth water. I haven't eaten a steak in ages. Okay, but you should know that the last time I played mini-golf was high school. I was awful then, and I'm sure I still am."

Who cared, as long as she said yes? He grinned. "Can't wait to see that."

~

SUMMER HADN'T SPOKEN with Dorie or Rainy since before the networking breakfast. She needed to catch them up, and simultaneous pedicures at Mai Lan's, a bustling nail business on the outskirts of town, had the space and equipment to accommodate three customers at the same time.

Plus the women who worked there, most of them Vietnamese and Korean, didn't gossip.

"I so needed this," Rainy said with a sigh as her feet soaked in a tub of warm, scented water.

"Same here." Dorie wriggled her toes. "Thanks to tax season sucking up all my time, my feet are a mess. Now that the weather has turned, I'm eager to wear sandals and flip-flops in public."

"I had my toes done before Sam and Adam's wedding," Summer said, "but then I had my little accident and the polish on my big toe got all messed up." She gestured at the badly chipped polish.

"I have lots to tell you," she added, while the manicurist trimmed and buffed her toenails to perfection. "Things for your ears only."

Dorie gave a sage nod. "I wondered why you picked this place instead of Tommie's."

The popular hair and nail salon was sure to be filled with people they knew, including Wanda, and possibly Betty Randall. Summer didn't want any of them poking around her private business.

"I also have things to share," Dorie said with a self-satisfied smile.

Had something finally happened with Paul? Summer rubbed her hands together. "That sounds juicy."

"My news is juicy in the worst way," Rainy muttered.

"What's happened?"

"Before I tell you, I want to hear what Dorie has to say."

The women working on their toes shook the bottles of polish each of them had selected. While they applied it in their quick, expert ways, Dorie shared. "I finally got up the nerve to invite Paul to have a drink with me after work last night."

"Way to go!" Summer arched her eyebrows. "And?"

"We had such a good time, we ended up ordering dinner. We talked until the place shut down around midnight. He walked me to my car and he kissed me good night."

"How was it?" Summer asked, remembering her first red-hot kiss with Tony in the women's bathroom.

"Not earth-shattering, but at least it happened."

"Nothing wrong with moving slowly." Rainy sounded dismal.

Again, Summer thought of Tony. When a man and woman couldn't keep their hands off each other, slow was impossible. Her entire body tingled in agreement. "When are you going to see him again?"

Dorie shrugged. "That ball is in his court."

They went quiet while the manicurists finished up and led them to the toe dryers.

"What's your news, Rainy?" Summer asked, enjoying the air on her feet.

"Brace yourself—it's a real downer. Might as well share it now and save your news for last. Dayton and I... We aren't going to live together or see each other anymore. We broke up."

Unable to believe her ears, Summer gaped at her sister. "When did that happen?"

"Thursday night." Rainy's eyes filled. Visibly struggling for control—she didn't like to cry in front of people any more than Summer did—she blinked the tears back.

"And you didn't you call me?" Summer asked, hurt.

Not that she would've answered. She'd been with Tony, going up in flames in spite of herself. Until Selena had dropped by.

"I couldn't call. It was too late at night and I was too upset. Besides, I had to get up and go to work yesterday."

"What happened?"

"Like I told you the day you took the kids to the movies, we hadn't been getting along."

"You wanted him to shoulder more of the rent on a bigger place."

"That's only part the problem. Maya and Hayden don't have their fathers or any strong male role models in their lives. They need to be around a man who cares about them. Dayton mostly ignores them. Then there's the way he looks at other women." Rainy made a sound of disgust. "It's disrespectful."

Summer knew firsthand about that.

"Guys look at women," Dorie said. "It's part of being male. They can't help themselves."

"But Dayton *really* checks them out, to the point of drooling, and he does it in front of me and the kids. I was too tired to cook dinner Thursday, so the four of us went out for fast food. If you could have seen him undressing the waitress with his eyes..."

Rainy scowled as she remembered. "She was as uncomfortable as I was. Anyway, after the kids went to bed, we had a huge fight. Dayton doesn't see anything wrong with what he did. I do, and I don't trust him anymore."

Summer didn't blame her. "I guess this means you're staying in your apartment."

"That's right. When I got home from work yesterday, he'd taken his stuff and left the key I gave him on the counter."

"Wish I could think of something to make you feel better. I hope you have something planned for the rest of the day."

"I'm going to clean the apartment from top to bottom, then watch a DVD with the kids and binge on junk food."

"That sounds fun. You're going to be fine. Putnam girls—" Summer waited for her sister to finish the chant.

"Refuse to lose," Rainy muttered, her shoulders slumping. "Tell me you have good news, Summer."

"Good and bad. First, the bad. My temp job ends Tuesday. I dread finding another, but that paycheck sure comes in handy. Which leads me to the good news..." Although Summer didn't see anyone she knew in the area, she lowered her voice. "I found a promising job lead." She explained about Jolynn and Renee's new company.

"After work yesterday I drove to their office, to see where they're located. While I was in the area, I decided I may as well remind them I exist. I dropped in for an impromptu tour. It's a nice office, and they seemed pleased that I stopped by. They hadn't heard from Malcolm. As soon as I left, I called him and asked him to contact them Monday morning."

Dorie beamed. "Look at you, taking charge of your future. You're such a mover and shaker."

"I'm jealous," Rainy said.

Summer reached over and squeezed her hand. "There's no reason why you can't take charge of your future."

"How do I do that?"

"For starters, don't let what happened with Dayton ruin your life. You're a wonderful person and you're smart. You don't need a man to be happy."

"Well, it sure helps."

Who could argue with that? Look at her own self, all warm and giddy at the thought of being with Tony this afternoon. Summer was almost as bubbly as the champagne that had jump-started whatever this thing between them was.

Okay, that made her nervous. She didn't need him in order to be happy, she reminded herself. She'd been perfectly happy without him.

"You're going to take the job, right?" Dorie asked.

"Tony asked me the same thing. As I told him, let's see if they make me an offer."

"Tony?" Her friend's eyes widened. "I had a hunch you'd change your mind about him."

"We're sort of seeing each other."

"Sort of? Either you are or you aren't."

"It means she is." For the first time that day, Rainy smiled. "Way to go, big sister."

Dorie grinned. "That man is too gorgeous not to get involved with."

"Don't get ahead of yourselves," Summer cautioned. "It's not serious. We're keeping things light and fun."

"I could use some light and fun," Rainy said. "When do you see him again?"

"After lunch. I've been driving myself insane—will they or will they not offer me a job, and if they do, will I take it? Tony needs to take his mind off his own problems, so we're getting together."

"What kind of problems?" Dorie said.

"His mother might be sick."

"Life-threatening sick?"

Tony hadn't told Summer not to talk about his mother's health, but he hadn't said she could, either. "She has symptoms that could mean a serious illness," she said, skipping over the details. "She had some tests, and she and Tony get the results Monday."

"I'd be scared," Rainy said. "Can you imagine how we'd feel if Shelley was going through something like that? Sure, she drives us nuts, but we love her."

In the silence that fell among them, Summer thanked her lucky stars that for all her mom's messed-up personal life, at least she was physically healthy. "Anyway, we both need to forget for a while."

"Gee, I wonder how you and Tony will do that?" Dorie deadpanned.

Summer rolled her eyes, but she'd been fantasizing quite a bit about the same thing. She wanted a repeat of their passionate time in the hotel, without alcohol or a sore foot. Not for the whole night, either. For what they wanted, a few hours would be enough.

The toe dryers shut off simultaneously.

Rainy checked her phone for the time. "We've been here over an hour, and I need to pick up the kids soon. They're at Shelley's, and you know how she is. If I leave them at her place for too long, she goes a little bonkers. Before I go, I want pictures of our toes to post on Facebook."

After snapping photos, they stopped at the front desk to pay.

"Is Tony taking you to dinner?" Rainy asked as they donned sunglasses and exited into the bright day.

Summer shook her head. "He's making something for us."

"He cooks, too? That's another thing Dayton never does—did." Rainy gave her head an envious shake. "Lucky you."

"You won't think so when you hear what we're doing first. Playing mini-golf."

"He'll be impressed by how bad you are." Her sister snorted. "You're the worst player ever."

"I warned him. If nothing else, he'll get a big laugh when he watches me miss the easy shots."

Outside, Summer hugged her sister and her friend. As she got in the car and buckled up, her stomach growled. Suddenly she was ravenous. Lately she sure had an appetite. Nerves, no doubt.

She drove straight to the nearest drive-thru for fish and chips, then went home to get ready for her date with Tony.

13

U p at dawn, Tony leashed Boomer and headed out for a run. The rising sun painted crimson streaks across the pale sky and birds twittered their greetings. The perfect start to a beautiful afternoon with Summer.

Mini-golf, a private barbecue, and after that...

He started thinking about her in his bed and tripped over a tree root. Only quick reflexes save him from falling flat on his face.

No more fantasizing about her during a run. "Sorry about that, Boom. Let's turn around and go home."

In the house, he gave his dog plenty of food and water. While the animal sated himself, Tony showered and dressed. After inhaling a couple bowls of cold cereal, he backed his flatbed out of the carport, unlocked the guardrail, and loaded up several dozen potted trees. He hauled them to two of the four nurseries that had contracted with him, then returned for the rest, which he delivered to the other two nurseries. Then he picked up enough pots and planting supplies for next spring's crops and returned home.

By the time he showered and changed clothes, it

was almost time to pick up Summer. He decided to touch base with his mother—a quick hello, as she worked Saturdays.

She picked up on the second ring. "Clark's Frames."

"Hey, Ma."

"Tony." She sounded pleased. "Aren't you sweet to call. You're in luck—it's been nonstop all morning, but at the moment we're quiet."

In the background he heard a female voice, no doubt her assistant, Ruby.

"Ruby says, 'Hi, handsome,' " his mother said.

She was his mom's age and happily married, but had always been a big flirt. "Tell her hi. How are you feeling?"

"Up and down. When I'm busy the pain doesn't bother me as much. I was going to call you. Do you want to come to Sunday dinner? I'll make that chicken casserole you like and a pan of brownies to share with the crew."

That didn't sound like a sick woman. Was she pulling the same old thing, only ramped up a notch? Tony hoped so. Anything was better than the Big C.

"Thanks for the invitation, but I wouldn't count on it."

"I know you like to have everything in order before you leave for work Monday morning, but surely you can get that all done before dinner tomorrow. When I go to the grocery later, I'll get Boomer some of those dog biscuits he likes," she cajoled, and the dog's sharp ears perked up. "It'd be nice to have company the night before I get my test results."

Tony's belly twisted and he scrubbed his hand over his face, but he didn't bite. "I would, but our community barbecue and fundraiser is the first of next month, and you wouldn't believe how much there is to do yet. Stuff that I can't work on during my regular shift that needs to be finalized by Monday."

"Can't you do that today?"

"Nope."

"Why not?"

"I have other plans."

"Such as?"

"You don't need to know."

His mother sucked in an audible breath. "You have a date. Who is she?"

He wasn't telling her squat. She found something wrong with every woman he dated. Always had. She'd never had one good thing to say about Charlotte, even before her personality flipped. Sure, she'd hired Summer to handle her taxes, but that and dating her were two different things.

"Uh-uh," he said. "You need to stay busy and keep your mind off those test results. Why don't you make plans to do something with Karen and Pat Sunday night? You always have a good time together."

"Don't try to change the subject. Tell me her name and I won't ask any more questions."

"I'll believe that never. Gotta go."

He disconnected. Boomer angled his head and seemed to frown, as in, For crying out loud, she's your mother.

"I know your game as well as I know hers—you want those dog treats."

In complete agreement, Boomer wriggled his hind end.

"Time for me to go." Whistling, Tony penned the boxer in the back with plenty of water. "Behave while I'm gone. When I get back, Summer will be with me. I'll share her with you, but only for a little while."

TONY PULLED up Summer's driveway right on time. The front door was open, no doubt to let in the fresh air. Balancing the carton he'd brought with him, he exited the CX, headed for the front porch, and peered through the screen.

"Hey," he called out.

"Hi, Tony! Be right there."

"What's that?" she asked, eyeing the twelve-pack of flower starts.

"These are for your window box. I picked them up when I dropped off an order earlier. By the end of the month, they'll be in full bloom."

"Aww, thanks. Are we planting them now?"

"They'll keep for a while, as long as you water them daily. Where do you want them?"

She pointed to a shady place under the living room window and he set the carton down.

He didn't really look at Summer until he brushed off his hands and stepped into her place. In snug denim shorts and a pink shirt that hugged her breasts, she looked hot. "Nice outfit."

Her gaze flashed over his cargos and T-shirt. "Yours, too." She started to step into her sandals, then paused and pointed at her feet. "I had a pedicure this morning. Do you like it?"

He liked everything about her. "Blue and gold, with stars on the big toes—cute."

"Wait'll you see them outside." On the way to his car moments later, she slipped out of one sandal, held onto his bicep and wriggled her toes so that they caught the sunlight. "Don't you love how the stars sparkle?"

"They're bright, all right. Good thing I'm wearing

my shades or they'd blind me."

Her laughter floated through the air and coaxed out his grin. "You're in a great mood," he said.

"This afternoon is about having fun, and I already am."

He opened the passenger door and she climbed in, her smooth, long legs making his mouth water. So beautiful. He put his hand on her thigh, leaned in, and kissed her. When he broke contact some moments later, she seemed dazed. "You're impossible to resist," he said, already wanting more.

Tearing himself away, he headed for the driver's side and got in.

"You'll change your tune when my golfing puts me to shame," Summer said. "I'll bet you're good at it."

"Not as good as I am on a regular course. Scratch that—I'm not that great anymore, but in college I was. I had to be, to keep my golf scholarship."

Her jaw dropped. "You went to college on a golf scholarship."

"It was the one sport I stuck with when my mom got sick."

"You could be out playing a real game with your friends. Why are you wasting time on a silly mini-golf game with me?"

"Because you're pretty and you smell nice. Plus, I like hanging with you."

She went all soft and tender before she turned skeptical. "There's fun and then there's bored, which is what you'll be when it takes me twenty tries to put the ball in the hole. I'm really bad."

"I doubt that."

Minutes into the game he changed his mind. "You can't be good at everything."

"And that's supposed to make me feel better?"

"You could use some pointers."

"Then please, take pity on me and share them."

There were no players behind them, so he gave her a quick lesson.

"Keep your eye on the target and aim the ball there."

"Like I'm not doing that now."

"You aren't—you glance down when you swing. Widen your stance. A little more. That's good. Let me see that golf swing."

"Um, I'm not sure what that should look like."

"Let me show you." He stepped behind her and covered her hands with his. Correction—she smelled better than nice, as sweet as a tropical garden.

"Now what?" she said, sounding slightly breathless.

"The hole is on the other side of the hill. Keep your eye on it when you swing."

She nodded, her hair tickling his chin and her behind dangerously close to his crotch. He cleared his throat. Guided her in the swing, then stepped away.

"So close!" she said, as excited as a kid who'd just learned to ride a bike.

"Now try again on your own. You're close enough to the hole that you don't need a full swing to put the ball in. Try a tap."

Using the same stance as before, she followed his instructions. The ball rolled into the cup. She did a little dance that had him chuckling.

"You laugh now, but you'd better watch out," she said. "I could end up beating you."

He got a kick out of her competitiveness. "Care to bet on that?"

"Okay. If I win, I get to pick the dessert for tonight."

Forget the cookies he'd bought. This was much

more interesting. He waggled his eyebrows. "What do you have in mind?"

"Not what you're thinking. You can take me to Giordano's Gelato. It's a new place on the south side."

"I haven't been yet."

"Well, I have and it's wicked good. They serve a sundae with a huge fudge cookie on the bottom, three scoops of gelato, and a caramel sauce that's killer."

He laughed. "You really like ice cream."

"Who doesn't? But this is *gelato*. It's similar to ice cream, but different."

"If you say so. What do I get if you lose?" he asked, cupping her hips and moving her close.

"I'll do the dishes."

"Is that all?" He went in for a kiss.

Giving him a dirty look, she batted him away. "Hey, we're in public and there are kids all over the place. We'll see."

Good enough. He grinned. "Lady, you got yourself a deal."

14

"**D**arn it, you trounced me," Summer wailed at the end of the mini-golf game. "I knew you would, but I so wanted an upset."

Tony's cocky grin should have annoyed her. Instead, she went weak with longing. She'd been simmering since he'd kissed her in the car.

"Hey, you learned fast and tried hard," he said. "That counts for something. I admire you."

"I'm flattered, but admiration won't get me a fudge cookie sundae."

"I'm no match for that pouty face. If you want it that bad, I'll take you over there after dinner."

"Yes!" She pumped her fist in the air just to see him grin. "For that, I'll do the dishes and help with the meal."

"We have a deal."

"I did something bold after work yesterday," Summer said as they ambled toward his car. "I paid a visit to Paley and Glick. They're in a brand-new building on the east side. They lease a suite on the top floor of a three-story building, with an option to lease added space as needed. Not counting the partners and the receptionist, there are only ten employees, and the pay isn't as much as it was at my old job. But the potential for growth is huge."

Tony nodded. "I'm familiar with the area. A couple years ago, I was in charge of inspecting the structures in the neighborhood. It's a mixed-use area—apartments, houses, and office buildings."

"My former boss promised to call them Monday and sing my praises." Summer let out a squeal, and Tony chuckled. He seemed to be having as much fun as she was.

"While they showed me around, we had a casual interview," she added. "They asked me questions, and I answered them. I think it went well, but who knows."

"I'm betting they'll offer you a job. I thought you were worried about the risks of working for a new company."

"I was, but between the tour and my pros and cons list... The pros way outnumber the cons."

"You made a list?"

"It's what I do when I have an important decision to make."

"If that works for you, cool."

"How do you make big decisions?"

"When I want something, I go after it."

His intense gaze set off all kinds of excitement in her most sensitive places. She shifted in her seat. "You don't think things through?"

"What's to think about? Either I want it or I don't." Silence and then, "You disapprove."

Realizing she was frowning, she hastened to explain. "My mother does it your way, and things usually go wrong for her."

"Maybe she doesn't know what she really wants. I don't act until I *know*."

Summer mulled that over. "Then you've probably made a list in your head."

"Never looked at it that way, but yeah." He drove toward the foothills of the Siskiyous, up a slight incline on a two-lane road that bisected lush woods. Slanting sunlight dappled the leaves in light and shadow.

"You live up here? I'm jealous. This is such a beautiful, magical place."

"Nothing can compare to the great outdoors. From my house, I can hike into the Siskiyou or to Guff's Lake."

"I don't hike, but if I spent much time up here, I would. Have you always lived this far from town?"

"It's not that far. I can get to the station in under thirty minutes. To answer your question, I rented an apartment near the firehouse for years. Around the time Charlotte and I split up some four years ago, I bought the cabin and a couple acres."

Summer pictured a small, rustic home nestled among the spruce and redwood trees. "Heck of a way to get over a breakup."

"That had nothing to do with buying my own place. I was tired of paying rent."

"I bought my house for the same reason."

"Back then, the property was dirt cheap. Today, I wouldn't be able to afford it."

"You were smart to buy when you did."

"At the time I didn't think about that. I just wanted to live up here." Slowing, he gestured at a turnoff she hadn't noticed. "This is it."

He rolled up a dirt driveway that had to be a quarter-mile long and eased into a double carport beside a battered flatbed truck. As she'd imagined, towering trees dotted the property. But the cabin she'd envisioned turned out to be a modern one-and-a-half-story home with natural wood siding.

"Some cabin," she said.

"After years of neglect, it wasn't fit to live in. I tore it down and built this."

"You built your own house?"

"No, but I did some of the work. My crewmates helped, too. Especially Rafe. He's had a lot of experience with construction."

Seriously wowed, she shook her head. "How long did it take?"

"From start to finish, about two years."

"You fight fires, play golf like a pro, and helped build your own house. I'm so impressed."

"Yeah?"

Tony's grin lit up his face and warmed Summer from the inside out. Had there ever been a more attractive man? She wanted to walk straight into his arms. Started to. Then Boomer barked.

"He's in the back and he's eager to see you." Tony reached for her hand. "Come on."

She liked how his fingers twined with hers. Liked him, period. It was a good thing they weren't going to get serious or she'd have been scared of her feelings.

At the rear of the house he opened the gate of the chain-link fence and gestured her into a huge yard.

She barely registered the neatly mowed lawn before Boomer barreled toward them, barking with excitement.

Grinning, Tony hunkered down. "Did you miss me, Boom?"

Ecstatic, the dog wriggled his rear end and licked Tony's face all over. When Tony straightened, Boomer repeated the welcome with Summer.

She couldn't help laughing. "I'm glad to see you, too."

When the dog trotted off, she looked around. Here there were fewer trees than in the front and a vast lawn. A sliding-glass door at the back of the house opened onto a brick patio with a table and chairs, the biggest lounger she'd ever seen, and a fancy grill. Past the patio on the far side of the yard was a doghouse. Along the opposite side, a greenhouse, a shed, and a second fence surrounded a large empty space that was mostly dirt.

"Is that where you grow your trees?" she asked, gesturing.

"I start them in the greenhouse in late fall and move them out here in the spring. The fence keeps Boomer from getting into trouble, doesn't it, Boom? How about a quick tour of the house. Then we'll start dinner."

Thanks to skylights and an abundance of windows, light filled the interior. Tony was as tidy as she was, everything clean and orderly. Masculine decor, dark, heavy furniture, and utilitarian blinds. A few paintings on white walls, and a great room with sofas and chairs, a stone fireplace, and an enormous flat-screen TV.

Impressive, but as impersonal as a vacation rental —except in the hallway that led to the kitchen, where photos filled the wall. In one, a grinning Tony and his crewmates posed in front the station. In another, he and several of the men proudly displayed fish they'd caught.

Summer stopped in front of the commendation that praised Tony for going above and beyond at a fire, which was framed along with his photo. No smiles here. Grimy, his expression somber and at the same time tender, he carried a crying toddler from a burning house to the boy's anxious parents.

"I remember that awful fire—the story was all over the news," she said. "It spread so fast that the little boy's parents barely escaped in time. They were distraught and fought to get back inside to rescue their son. You're the firefighter who saved him. You really are a hero."

He gave a modest shrug. "Just doing my job."

Such humility. Summer's respect for him grew. "I'm in awe. Tony Clark, you're an amazing man."

"Keep saying that and I'll get a swelled head."

Doubtful. He was decent and modest and obviously dedicated to keeping people safe.

"This way to the kitchen," he said, nodding ahead.

The kitchen was marginally smaller than the great room. "This is as big as my kitchen, living room, and bedroom combined," she marveled. "You have enough room to cook and put a table."

"I like space."

"So I see."

As they returned to the great room, she pointed at the spiral staircase. "When we got here I noticed the balcony up there. Is that where your bedroom is?"

"Yes." His eyes glittered. "Wait till you see the view."

He led her up the staircase. She went straight to the windows along the balcony. "Mind if we go outside?"

"Not at all."

An instant later, she stood at the waist-high safety wall. "You're right about this view. I can see past the woods, all the way to the mountains."

"It's nice, all right. For another great view, check this out."

Inside again, he gestured above the king-size bed.

Summer glanced upward. "That's the biggest skylight I've ever seen."

"I enjoy looking at the sky when I'm in bed. Care to test it out?"

She angled him a look. "Are you trying to seduce me, Mr. Clark?"

"Oh, yeah." Flashing a wicked grin, he crooked his finger and beckoned her over.

"You had me at skylight." She stepped into his arms.

~

TONY HAULED Summer up nice and close, and kissed her until he was about to ignite. He tore his mouth from hers. "Sweet Jesus, I want you."

Her eyelids fluttered open. "Then you're in luck—I'm all yours."

Her dazed expression ramped up his hunger. Their shirts disappeared. Her breasts swelled against her bra, a skimpy lace thing made to tantalize.

"You look sexy." He did some tantalizing of his own, toying with her nipples.

Gasping, she gripped his shoulders. "I knew this bra would turn you on."

"Sweetheart, if you were covered from head to toe in armor, you'd turn me on."

"Spoken like a red-blooded man."

"That I am." He slid his hands down her sides, playing with the button of her shorts. "We do have a problem, though."

"What's that?" She sounded breathless.

"For what I have planned, I need you naked."

Seconds later, she lay nude on his bed, flushed and

ready for what they both wanted. The raw desire on her face almost brought him to his knees.

As eager as he was to make her his, he stood over her.

"What are you doing?" she asked, clearly impatient.

"Looking at you."

"Oh." Indulging him, she stretched her arms out and arched her back so that her breasts jutted up.

He sucked in a breath. "You're so beautiful."

"What I am is frustrated." She reached for him. "Get down here now."

He gave a low laugh. "Bossy, aren't you?"

And impossible to resist. With lightning speed, he joined her. Took her mouth, then tasted his way down her body, her every moan bringing him closer to losing control. He flirted with her most sensitive place, made her writhe and beg, then put his mouth on her. She grasped his ears and held him there. Sensing she was about to climax, he raised his head. "Don't let go yet, Summer. When you do, I want to be inside you."

"Then you'd better hurry."

He paused to roll on a condom, then returned back to her. One thrust and he was where he wanted to be—gloved in her moist heat, and using every ounce of strength he possessed to fight for control.

"Finally," she sighed, and gripped his hips with her thighs.

She squeezed the muscles in another place and his control slipped. "Easy," he groaned, wanting to prolong the pleasure. He lost that battle. Sweating and shuddering, he went over the edge with her.

Afterward, unable to move, he remained buried in her. Finally he propped himself on his arms, brushed her hair from her face, and gave her a quick kiss. "I sure am happy you changed your mind about us."

"Me, too." Her satiated smile mirrored his own.

She started to slide her hands up his torso, then frowned. "Your back is all scratched up. Did I do that?"

"You raked your nails over me, yeah."

"Raked? Jeesh. I guess there's a first time for everything."

"Second—you did the same thing at the hotel." He grinned.

She looked shocked. "I guess I got carried away. Sorry."

"I don't mind. Unleashing your passion is my new favorite thing. Plus, I like being the first man to carry you away like that." He rolled over beside her and pointed at the skylight. "Great view, huh?"

"Now that you're not distracting me, I can actually focus on that. Look at the puffy little clouds moving past. Do you see the one that looks like a lamb?"

"What I see is a tiger's head. You turn me into a tiger." He nuzzled the crook of her neck, and she laughed.

"I'm all tigered out, hot stuff."

"Me, too—for now. You should see the stars at night." He thought about asking her to stay over, but spending a full night with a woman wasn't his style. With the exception of the night at the hotel, an alcohol-infused fluke.

No comment from her either, although she suddenly seemed on edge, as if waiting for something. Damn, did she expect an invitation? She wasn't going to get one. In no mood to get into that now, he tabled the conversation until later, before he drove to the gelato place. They'd eat their desserts there, then he'd take her home.

Time to get out of bed. "Notice that the sky is considerably paler than when we came up here," he said. "You know what that means."

"That we've been busy for a while?"

"That, too." He kicked off his covers and sat up. "It's almost dinnertime. I don't know about you, but I'm getting hungry for those steaks."

"So am I." Covering herself with the blanket—as if he hadn't feasted his eyes on every mouth-watering inch of her body—she sat up beside him. "I need the bathroom."

"Help yourself." He pointed at the master off his bedroom. "If you want a shower, the towels in there are clean."

"All right, but don't *you* want to shower?"

Yeah, but he needed his space. He swung his legs over the bed. "A bathroom is a bathroom. I'll use the one downstairs and meet you in the kitchen."

15

Tony's bathroom also had a skylight, over the shower. Not as impressive as the one above his bed, Summer thought as she dressed, but pretty darned cool. He'd mentioned lying in bed at night and looking at the sky.

The sun wouldn't set for several hours, with complete darkness falling even later. Did he plan for her to be here that long? To stay over? He'd almost sounded as if he did, which made her nervous.

True, they'd already spent a full night together, but that'd been a one-time thing. They'd also decided not to have sex again—or she had—until she'd changed her mind... She wasn't one bit sorry and wouldn't mind more.

But waking up beside him in the morning seemed way too serious for the kind of relationship they both wanted. To her, anyway. She wasn't sure about Tony. Did he expect his lovers, expect her, to stay over?

Probably not. Standing in front of the mirror, she smoothed her hair. "He doesn't want me in his bed all night," she told herself.

Yet she headed downstairs feeling apprehensive.

In the kitchen, he was sliding potatoes in the oven to bake. "Hey."

He flashed the lazy grin she'd grown used to, nothing especially meaningful or tender, easing some of her misgivings. They'd had fun in bed. Otherwise, nothing had changed between them. But to be sure, if the subject came up she'd set him straight. If it didn't, at some point after the meal she'd plead exhaustion and ask him to take her home.

"What can I do to help?" she asked.

"How about putting a salad together while I whip up my special steak sauce." She nodded and he gestured at a drawer under the counter. "Aprons are in there and salad fixings are in the fridge. Use any bowl from the cabinet under the island table."

In no time, they stood across from each other at the island, Summer chopping and filling a bowl with crisp lettuce, and Tony adding spices to oil and melted butter.

"That sauce already looks yummy. What else goes in there?" she asked, peering at the spice containers.

"Avert your eyes, woman. This is a secret recipe."

"Now I'm really curious. Pretty please, let me look? I won't reveal a thing to anyone, I promise."

"Prove I can trust you." Except for the humorous glint in his eyes he looked dead serious.

"What do I have to do?"

"Plant a big one right here." He pointed at his mouth.

"If I must." Fighting a smile, she rounded the island, stood on her toes, and pulled his head down.

"You look hot in that apron. I'm picturing you wearing nothing but."

She opened her mouth with a sassy retort, but he

cupped her bottom in his big hands and lifted her for a sizzling kiss.

She forgot her wariness and what she'd been about to say, forgot everything but him.

"You passed the test," he said when he released her sometime later.

What test? For the life of her, she couldn't remember.

"Feel free to check out the ingredients I use."

That's right—the steak sauce. She squinted at the labels. So many good spices. "I can't wait to try it."

The kiss and working on dinner together further relaxed her. "When I was little, I dreamed of a kitchen like this," she said as she sliced a green pepper. "A place where a real family gathers for meals."

"Define a 'real' family."

"One with a mom and a dad. I imagined Rainy and me eating breakfast and dinner with both of them."

"Two parents at the same table isn't necessarily a good thing."

"I would've liked the chance to find out."

"That's right, yours divorced before you were born."

"And yours were married eighteen years."

"Eighteen hellish years."

"You said that before, but I can't believe their relationship was bad the entire time."

"Maybe not, but I don't remember them ever getting along."

"They argued a lot?"

"Mostly my mother nagged my father. She was always on him for something. He hated that. I didn't enjoy it, either. He traveled for business, and the more she nagged the longer he stayed away. The last few years before the divorce he was gone most of the time."

"That must've been hard on you and your mom."

"The tension between them was no picnic, either. When she was diagnosed with cancer..." Tony shook his head.

"He didn't even come back then?"

"Not often."

"But I assumed... Who took her to the doctor?"

"Friends, if she had an appointment when I was in class. Otherwise, I drove her. I sat with her during chemo and when she puked her guts out after."

Summer's esteem for him grew by leaps. "You were only sixteen."

"Someone had to be there for her."

"I'm sure she's grateful for what you did."

"All I know is, she began to depend on me more than ever. That was hard. She'd always been possessive, insisting I spend most of my spare time with her. She didn't like sharing me with my guy friends, and forget girlfriends. Before the cancer, I pretty much ignored her complaints. After, I stayed home with her."

Summer couldn't imagine. "You went through some really difficult times."

"Everyone has burdens. Despite my responsibilities, I still managed to have a life."

"At least she isn't that way anymore."

"Don't bet on it. She's still trying to control me, so I don't tell her much." He reached across the island, grabbed a slice of green pepper, and popped it in his mouth.

Summer batted him away. "My mom was the opposite, always eager to get rid of us, especially when she had a new man in her life."

"That doesn't sound half-bad to me."

"Funny—I was thinking the same thing about your situation."

"The grass is always greener, and all that." Finished, Tony whisked the sauce ingredients until they were blended. "In spite of the challenges we both grew up with, we survived."

Proud of all she'd accomplished despite the odds, Summer raised her chin. "We did a lot better than that." She wiped her hands on her apron and took it off. "All done."

"Just in time to fire up the grill. You grab the wine to drink and I'll carry the steaks. Mind if we eat outside tonight?"

"I'd love that, but I'll pass on the wine."

"How about a beer?"

Summer shook her head. "This is going to sound weird, but since Sam and Adam's wedding I've lost my taste for alcohol. Do you have soda pop?"

Minutes later, holding the drinks, she followed Tony to the patio, her eyes on his very fine butt as he carried the steaks and sauce.

STILL TASTING the spicy flavors on her tongue, Summer sat back in her patio chair and licked her lips. "You weren't kidding about the sauce—that steak was out of this world."

Tony beamed. "What'd I tell you. You made Boomer real happy with the bone you gave him."

"Where'd he go, anyway?"

"He likes to take his scraps to his dog house. It'll be dark soon."

"No more warm sun." She glanced at the sky and rubbed her arms.

"Cold?" he asked.

"A little. I wish I'd thought to bring a sweater."

"It's cooler up here at night than it is in town. I'll warm you up." He grabbed her hand and led her to the double chaise, which had a fleece throw flung across it. "We'll cover up with this blanket, look at the stars, and digest."

"Okay, but I don't want to stay too late." She caught her breath and waited for his reaction.

"No prob. The gelato place probably closes around ten. We'll stop there, then I'll take you home. Scoot over."

He didn't want her to stay. The tension whooshed out of her.

He lay down beside her, the chaise creaking, and put his arm around her shoulders. With his other arm, he covered them with the blanket. "Good?"

Tony was warmer than any blanket. "I'm not cold anymore. Your double chaise is nice, but you're a big man and it's kinda crowded for two."

"I like crowded."

"Earlier you said you like space."

"In my house, not out here with you." He gave her a kiss that was all too brief. "What's on your agenda tomorrow?"

"Cleaning house, laundry, grocery shopping—all the chores that didn't get done today. You?"

"I have chores, too, plus Nate and I are meeting to iron out the details of the fundraiser and barbecue that need to be finalized by Monday."

"You're doing a ton of planning."

"Which will pay off big time. After that I'll stop by my mom's. She's nervous about getting those test results and I want to calm her down."

"You're awfully good to her. Even if she does try to control you."

He pointed up. "Look."

"I finally see stars."

"Just you wait. We don't get much light pollution in the foothills, and with a new moon tonight... You're in for a treat that will rock your world."

As the night deepened, stars flooded the sky. "I had no idea there were so many," Summer marveled. "Unbelievable."

"You're joking."

She shook her head. "I took an astronomy class in college, but I never realized so much was visible to the naked eye."

"You've never been camping? We need to rectify that."

"No, we don't. Right here, right now is outdoorsy enough for me. No wonder you installed that huge skylight over your bed."

"Showing you the sky as it really is and seeing your wonder firsthand—it doesn't get any better than this."

"I'll bet you say that to all the girls you invite to dinner."

"You're the first I've cooked for since I moved in."

"You expect me to believe that?" she teased, but she wanted to know.

"It's the truth."

He'd never looked at her with such tenderness. That worried her. *Please, don't let him have serious feelings for me.* Nervous all over again, she tensed.

Oblivious, he caressed her bare arm, kissed the top of her head. "Having a good time?"

"It's been a great day. I haven't thought about Paley and Glick in hours."

"Haven't thought about my mom, either, except when I told you about growing up. You and I... We're good for each other. We should do this again soon."

"As long as... We're keeping our relationship light and fun, yes?"

"That's the plan."

She was relieved to hear that. Lying here with Tony, staring up at the brilliant stars, was romantic and cozy. After the long week, full day, and large meal, she grew drowsy. She was on the verge of drifting off when he nudged her.

"Uh-uh, don't you go to sleep on me."

"But I'm tired." She burrowed into his warmth.

"I know a great way to wake you up." He tipped up her chin and grinned. "Wanna mess around?"

"Out here? What if someone sees us?"

"No one will. My nearest neighbor is on the other side of the woods, almost a mile away. It's just you, me, and the stars."

He tilted her chin and kissed her. The fatigue left her. Before long, his hands were everywhere, stoking the fire inside. She wanted him so much, she shivered.

"Still cold?" he asked.

"The opposite—I'm burning up. For you." She pulled him into another searing kiss.

Before long they were both naked on the chaise. Out-of-her-mind ravenous for him, Summer pressed her thigh to his hips.

"Your passion turns me on," he said.

"It'd better, because I need you inside me. Please tell me we don't have to stop so you can go get protection."

He let out the low laugh that sparked all her sensitive places. "I happen to have a couple packets in one of the pockets of my cargos."

"Planned for this, did you?"

"Around you, I'm always prepared." Reaching

down beside him where he'd tossed his clothes, he fished a packet out and tore open the foil.

Summer stopped him from putting the condom on. "I'll take it from here."

She rolled it down slowly, enjoying the hiss of his breath and the corded muscles in his arms as he gripped the cushions of the chaise.

"All done," she said.

He started to sit up but she pushed him down. "Stay right where you are."

"You're the boss."

"That's the way I like it." She climbed over him. Eased down a little, teasing him and herself. Tony raised his hips. She raised higher. "Patience, Tony. Oh, the sweet revenge of making you wait. Payback can be hard. And you're so very, very hard—"

Suddenly she found herself on her back, coming apart while he drove into her over and over, until he called out her name and she lost herself in release.

Later, both on their backs, he curled his palm around her hip. "Damn, we're good together."

"The best." Summer stared up at the glittering sky. "Looking up there, I feel so small."

"Sure puts things into perspective."

"In what way?"

"The universe is too big to wrap our minds around, and here we are, stressing over silly little things. Whether we made a mistake or gave a wrong answer or forgot the eggs at the store. When I study the sky, I'm reminded not to sweat the small stuff."

"I sweat over the small stuff, the big stuff, and everything in between."

"Are you doing that now, Summer?"

She shook her head. "I'm too relaxed and I feel too wonderful for that."

"Ditto. That was our goal today—to take our minds off our troubles. Our work here is done."

Those words were the last thing Summer remembered until later, when Tony gently shook her. "We fell asleep."

She burrowed closer. "Give me another hour? I'm too tired to move."

True to his word, he woke her. "It's after two. If you want to move upstairs for what's left of the night... But I have a lot to do tomorrow."

And Summer wanted to finish out the night in her own bed, by herself. "I'm ready to go home."

He let out what seemed a relieved breath. "Let's get dressed."

16

"We never made it to Giordano's," Summer said around a yawn as Tony pulled into her driveway.

His own yawn followed. They were both dead tired. "Next time for sure."

"You don't understand. I've been thinking about that sundae since mini-golf. I don't just want it, I crave it." She licked her lips and rubbed her stomach. "As exhausted as I am, if the gelato place was open at this hour I'd seriously consider driving over there."

"Man, you're impatient. Why didn't I know this about you before?"

"I am not—except when I have my heart set on something. Then I want it as soon as possible."

"Which is the definition of the word."

"If that were true, I'd never have lasted as a CPA."

"All right, in some areas of your life, you show patience. Not about getting your gelato and definitely not in bed."

She did a provocative pose, thrusting her breasts forward, pursing her lips, and giving her head a saucy shake. "That's your fault—you push all my hot buttons."

He let out a growl of pleasure. "Back at ya. When you're all worked up, so am I."

Reaching out, he hauled her as close as possible given the console and kissed her. With a sigh, she wrapped her arms around his neck.

His hunger rose up sharp and fierce. He considered inviting himself in, but they both needed space. With reluctance, he released her. "Sleep tight, and we'll get that gelato soon."

AFTER TONY and Nate nailed down the activities for the barbecue Sunday afternoon, he headed to his mom's.

"You should have called to tell me you were coming," she said. "I took your advice and made dinner plans with Karen and Pat, and I have to leave in ten minutes."

"I can't stay long, anyway. Consider this a quick visit to check in. Good for you, going out with your friends and having a good time."

She smiled.

"How are you feeling?" he asked.

"Pretty good at the moment."

A big relief. "You look great."

"Thank you, Tony. So do you." She gave him a sly look. "The date you had yesterday must've agreed with you."

And then some. He was still jazzed from being with Summer and eager to see her again. "We had fun."

"Where did you go, and what did you do?"

He shook his head. "Stop, Ma."

"You can't blame me for wanting to know, but all

right." She sighed. "I just—I want so much to see you settled before I die."

His gut clenched. "You're not going to die anytime soon."

"We'll see what the test results say."

Manipulative or not, he couldn't leave her like this. "Listen, if you need me to stick around for a while..."

"No, son. Karen and Pat are expecting me. I made those brownies for you and the rest of the crew and bought Boomer's favorite biscuits. "

"That's real sweet. What time will Dr. Geddes call?" he asked as she handed him a plastic bin filled with brownies and a the package of dog treats.

"She didn't say. I'm sure I'll hear from her as soon as she gets the test results."

He kissed her cheek. "Phone me immediately. If I'm out on a call, leave a message. I'll get back to you as soon as possible. And enjoy yourself tonight."

"I plan to," she said, her hands twisting at her waist.

"It'll be okay," he assured her. And hoped to God he was right.

17

After sleeping in on Sunday morning, the first time in weeks, Summer lay in bed with a smile on her face. Thanks to her amazing date with Tony, she'd forgotten her worries for a while. She felt rested and content, her mind and body for once in sync.

Besides being a fantastic lover, he gave her cool presents. No other man had brought her an ice cream cone or flower starts.

Best of all, he was all hers.

For now.

Who knew a light and fun relationship would work out so well? Humming, she started a load of laundry, cleaned house, and puttered around. It was a beautiful, warm day, and late in the afternoon she headed outside to transplant the tiny flower shoots. A pamphlet in the carton explained what kind they were and how to care for them.

She spent an enjoyable time planting them in the window box, then carefully watering the roots. When she finished, she brushed the dirt off her hands and stood back to admire her work. Not much to see yet, but in a few weeks...

By then, assuming she got the job offer and assuming she accepted it, she'd have a new position as a senior manager. As exciting as that possibility was, suddenly she feel queasy, even if her pros and cons list was stacked in favor of taking the position at Paley and Glick.

Summer shook her head. There she went, sweating the small stuff. Or maybe she was hungry. She hadn't eaten since lunch, and here it was, almost time for dinner. After making a tuna sandwich and grabbing a bag of chips, she took her plate to the front porch and sat down to enjoy the slanting rays of the sun. While she ate she daydreamed about Tony, half-wishing he was here now.

Suddenly, as if she'd conjured him up, he pulled into the driveway.

Seconds later he exited the CX, leashed Boomer, and let him out. Barking with excitement, the dog strained at his leash. Toting a large plastic container in his free hand, Tony strode toward her in all his gorgeous glory.

Her heart did a happy dance in her chest. "Hi, there," she said. "I was just thinking about you."

"Yeah?" His bad-boy grin lit her up inside.

"Not you—Boomer." She gave the dog a hug, then eyed the package in Tony's hands. "What'd you bring me this time?"

"Brownies. My mom baked them for me and my crewmates, but I figured you deserved a couple. Seeing as how you didn't get that gelato last night."

"Yum. This almost makes up for that. Let me grab some napkins and lemonade." Summer stood.

Tony's gaze drifted over her shorts and sleeveless top. He made a pleased sound. "Nice outfit."

Faded cutoffs and a tank streaked with dirt? She

lifted her hair off her neck. "I'm trying to stay cool. It's warm tonight."

His smoldering eyes didn't help. "Sure is."

"I'll be back."

When she returned to the front porch, Tony was sitting where she'd been, propped on his arms with his ankles crossed. Looking like a man without a care in the world.

She handed him an icy lemonade, nudged him over and sat down beside him. Then she helped herself to a brownie. "OMG, these are amazing! Your mother is a fantastic cook. Does she know you're here?"

"Hell, I didn't even know I was coming. I spent the afternoon working on that community event, then dropped by to see her. I was on my way home from grabbing a quick burger, but the car brought me here instead. Go figure."

Summer was way too happy about that. "I didn't expect to see you again till after your double shift."

"Forty-eight hours is a long time to be without you."

She went hot inside.

"Plus, my mom gets those test results tomorrow and you're waiting to hear about the job... We both need to take our minds off our problems."

"That's for sure." Summer gestured at the window box. "I planted the flower starts. The information sheet says they like sun."

"In that box, they'll get it. Hey, do you want to come to our event? There'll be a barbecue and some good fun."

"I don't work for the fire department."

"We sponsor it, but the entire community is invited. My crewmates are bringing their wives or girlfriends, and I'd like you to be my date. You'll have to bring yourself but we'll eat together and I'll hang with you when I can."

"I'm not your girlfriend."

"No, but we're seeing each other." He leaned down and kissed her.

She started to sink against him, then came to her senses. "Not out here. Unlike your neighborhood, mine is filled with nosy people."

"Selena—I forgot."

"And everyone else."

"None of them will care if I kiss you."

"I care. My love life is private."

"Then let's go inside." He called Boomer over, rose and gave her a hand up.

In the house, he locked the screen, and closed and dead-bolted the door. He backed her against the same door, slid his hands up the back of her head, and pressed nice and close for a deep, hungry kiss. All on its own, her leg gripped his thighs, bringing him closer still to where she most wanted him.

When they broke apart they were both breathing hard and she was ready to pull off her clothes and his. He rested his forehead against hers. "I've been thinking about that since this morning."

Too dazed to play games, she sighed. "Me, too."

"I happen to have several condoms in my pocket." He rubbed her nipple with his finger. "Let's go to bed."

Pleasure and hunger rippled through her. "All right, but you can't stay late. You have work tomorrow and I have two more days at the temp job."

"What I have in mind won't take long."

He was right—there was nothing slow about their lovemaking. Wild for him, she matched his urgency in every way. As quickly as they came together, the sex was every bit as delicious as the night before.

Relaxed and sated, Summer snuggled next to him and fell asleep with her head on his chest.

Sometime later she woke up. By Tony's even breathing, he was in dreamland. She elbowed him. "For the life of me, I can't see the clock. Where is it?"

"Hell if I know." After a minute, he chuckled. "No wonder—your shirt is draped over it." He tossed it aside. "It's a few minutes after ten. I should shower before I go, so I won't have to in the morning. Join me and you won't have to rush tomorrow, either."

"I've never showered at night."

"Try it, you'll like it."

"You're right," she purred sometime later. "That was the best shower sex of my life."

"Told you." He wrapped her in a towel and carried her back to bed.

He leaned down to kiss her, then gave up and joined her. "I can't get enough of you."

After another sizzling kiss, she smiled. "This is going to ruin your plan for skipping a shower in the morning."

"It's worth the hassle."

In full agreement, she welcomed him. They fell back to sleep for a while.

This time, he woke her. "It's one a.m."

She wasn't ready for him to go. "Do you have to leave?"

"Not yet. I can handle staying awhile if you can."

They were both tired. "You need your rest and so do I," she reasoned. "Another hour can't hurt."

She woke again when he shook the covers off his side of the bed. "What time is it?"

"Later than we planned—almost five."

Basically all night. While that sank in, he left her bed. "I have to get home, pack my stuff for work, and drop Boomer at the dog sitter's by 7:30."

"I should get up soon, too."

Summer flipped on the bedside table lamp and watched him dress. He wasn't at all self-conscious, sliding his long, muscled legs into his boxers and cargos, and pulling on his T-shirt.

He grinned. "You're checking me out like you don't know what's under here."

"Believe me, I know. Don't let this go to your head, but with or without your clothes you're one sexy man." She could stare at him all day and never grow bored.

"Back at ya." The heat of his hungry gaze sizzled through her. "If I didn't have to go, I'd crawl right back into bed and ravish you again."

"Toss me my robe—it's hanging on a hook in my closet—and I'll walk you to the door."

"I hope your day will go by fast," he said as he stood in the threshold.

"You and me both. Keep me updated on your mom."

"I'll call when I can. If things are crazy, I'll text."

He kissed her and left.

He was such a large presence, filling the house with his energy. With him and Boomer gone, the place seemed eerily silent. Almost...lonely.

Having always valued solitude—for most of her life she'd depended on alone time to recharge—Summer wasn't sure what to make of that. She wasn't ready for deep feelings. Neither was Tony.

We're enjoying each other for as long as it lasts—that's all, she assured herself as she scooped up her clothes and dropped them in the hamper on the way to the bathroom.

Mentally prepping for the tedious day ahead, she stepped into the shower again.

Summer's second to last day as a receptionist was as quiet and slow as she'd envisioned, giving her way too much time to stew. In a few short weeks, the second and final severance payment would be deposited in her bank account. After that...

Bile rose in her throat, and she swallowed against the fear. Forget waiting for a job offer from Paley and Glick. She needed work now.

Unfortunately, finding an accounting job in late May was proving impossible, which left her with accepting another temp position or taking a job as a cocktail waitress or a restaurant server. None of those options excited her, but any job was better than none.

After taking a coffee break she checked online for new job postings—for the second time today—in case something new had been posted. Nothing had. Time to suck it up and call the temp agency. As she reached for her cell phone it rang. Paley and Glick.

Sucking in a calming breath, she answered. Jolynn greeted her. After the usual small talk, during which Summer wanted to pull out her hair, the woman got to the point of the call.

"We heard from Malcolm Tillinger."

"Oh, good." Summer crossed her fingers that her old boss had given her the glowing reference he'd promised.

"He had great things to say about you. Now we'd like to schedule a formal interview."

Yes!

"Are you available sometime this week?" Jolynn asked

"Let me check my calendar." As if Summer needed to. Aside from her last day of work tomorrow and likely seeing Tony when his shift ended, her schedule was wide open.

When she disconnected, she had an interview set up for Wednesday. Hot damn!

She couldn't wait to tell Tony. At nearly ten-thirty he was likely busy, putting out fires or doing any number of the things firefighters did. She didn't expect him to answer, but to her surprise, he picked up.

"Hey," he said, using his low, intimate voice. "I was just thinking about you. I sure enjoyed last night."

"Me, too."

In the quiet moment that followed, memories of the passion and pleasure they'd shared washed over her. Her well-loved body began to hum and ache for him. She crossed her legs, which didn't help at all.

"Summer? You still there?"

"I'm here. I thought sure I'd have to leave a message. You're usually swamped."

"It's slow this morning. I'm on my way to work out at our upstairs gym with a couple of my crewmates. I have about two minutes to talk. What's up?"

"Guess who has an interview at Paley and Glick Wednesday?"

"Atta girl. Blow them away, and keep me informed."

"I will, and you do the same with your mom."

18

I t'd been a full week since Tony and his crewmates had worked out together at the gym on the second floor of the firehouse, and competition to outdo each other was fierce. Near the end of a rigorous session, Tony was sweating and feeling good.

"Any word on your mom?" Nate asked, mopping his face with a towel.

"Nothing yet. She'll call when she hears from her doctor."

Nate nodded. "For a guy with that hanging over you, you're in a decent mood. I doubt this workout is responsible. How's Summer?"

"Fantastic. I saw her over the weekend."

"Look at you, grinning like a fool. I haven't seen you like this over a female since...never."

"We get along great. She's different from the women I usually date."

"A class act," Rafe agreed.

Owen, the resident geek, nodded. "Smart, too." He sniffed his armpits and made a face. "I need a shower."

Didn't they all. After cleaning up they clomped toward the kitchen for snacks and water.

"This is the first time in a while that you've had a girlfriend," Ethan said on the way. "Is she coming to the barbecue?"

"I don't do girlfriends," Tony reminded him. "But yeah, I invited her."

She hadn't said whether she'd make it, mainly because they'd gotten distracted with each other and then had forgotten everything else.

Nate gave him a speculative look. "You sure are seeing a lot of your non-girlfriend."

"So?" Summer made him feel better about his mom's health issues. Hell, when he was with her the whole world seemed brighter.

"You're really into her."

"She likes me, too. We get along so well because neither of us is looking for promises or commitments. She has a job interview Wednesday."

A couple of guys nodded and told Tony to wish her good luck.

While Tony guzzled water, the alarm sounded, and Sarah McCone, the dispatcher, announced a fire at a construction site.

Within minutes he and the other crewmates assigned to the fire engine had stepped into their fire-resistant clothing, boarded, and buckled in. The three men on paramedic duty jumped into the aid car and followed them out.

The fire, a kitchen mishap gone awry, was the first of a string of emergencies. A three-car collision and resulting car fire, an overturned semi sending ominous smoke over the road and adjacent field, and a false alarm. Tony barely had time to cram a sandwich into his mouth, let alone think about his mother.

She called while he was out saving lives and

fighting fires, and he didn't have time to call her back until late in the afternoon, when things finally slowed down. Wandering outside, he leaned against the station wall and phoned her.

"Tell me."

"Hi, son. I explained everything in my voice message. Didn't you listen to it?"

She sounded upbeat, but he needed to know. "I'd rather hear it from you now."

When he disconnected, he wore a grin.

MONDAY AFTERNOON SUMMER waltzed out the door of the accounting firm. One more day and then... The interview with Jolynn and Renee! As she crossed the parking lot her phone rang. Tony.

"Hey," he said. "Still excited about that job interview?"

"Way too much."

"Nothing wrong with good ol' enthusiasm."

"An interview is no guarantee of anything."

"You'll get the job."

He believed in her—but then, he always had. Although he couldn't see her, she smiled. "Thanks for the vote of confidence. You have no idea how great it feels to be wanted."

"You're wanted, all right."

His low growl vibrated through her body, and she moaned. "If you're trying to turn me on, it's working."

"Yeah? Where are you?"

"Heading to my car. What did you have in mind?"

"Sadly, not that. I heard from my mom. Good news —no cancer."

Summer was beyond relieved. "Thank God. Did her doctor figure out why she's been feeling bad?"

"Yep—benign cysts and a bad case of acid reflux heightened by stress."

"Stress from what?"

"Working herself up with worry. Dr. Geddes prescribed a medication that should help. She needs to clean up her diet, too. More vegetables, less fried food, fewer sweets. The doc suggested she take a daily walk or sign up for an exercise class, but with her long days at Clark's Frames... I can't see her doing either unless she cuts her hours back."

"Surely some of her employees can fill in."

"She's always insisted on running every detail of the business, but most of her staff has been with her for years. It's time she trusted them to take over part of the load."

"Being that way myself, I understand. What about the cysts?"

"There's a possibility they'll go away on their own, but she can help that along by drinking more water and limiting herself to decaf coffee or herbal tea."

"Your poor mom! I couldn't survive without caffeine."

"Hey, if it gets rid of the cysts... Otherwise, she'll have to go under the surgeon's knife to remove them."

"What a choice."

"Not fun, for sure. Did you know all women are supposed to examine their breasts for lumps?"

"Yes, and I try, but I don't always remember."

"Anytime you need a breast check, I'm available."

Summer's nipples perked up. "Yes, please, Dr. Clark."

"I'll schedule you an appointment ASAP."

"You're such a tease." She unlocked her car and got in.

"I mean it. Next time I see you, I'll give you a thorough checkup. How about Wednesday night? I meant to tell you yesterday that I leave Thursday for a fishing trip with Nate, Hank, and Max. We'll be back Saturday."

"And a good thing, with Mother's Day on Sunday." Whether or not Summer got a job offer, she wanted another night with Tony. "I'll text when I'm home after the interview."

"Good plan. My mom wants to go to Rosemary's for Mother's Day. I made a reservation—the only day of the year the restaurant takes reservations."

"That's where Rainy and I are taking Shelley." At the thought of seeing Tony there, Summer groaned. "I don't think it's a good idea for us to run into each other when we're with our mothers."

"I'm with you on that. Mine keeps bugging me about the 'mystery woman' I'm dating. What time is your reservation?"

"Ten-thirty."

"Ours is at nine. By the time you show up we'll be long gone."

"Whew," Summer said. "Crisis averted."

"Hey, you never said if you'll come to the community barbecue."

"That's not for another three weeks."

"So? You like to plan ahead."

"You know me well." She laughed. "Since you'll be busy and we'll come in separate cars, can I bring Rainy and the kids? She and her boyfriend broke up and she needs something fun to look forward to."

"You bet. Like I said, this event is for the whole community."

"Then yes, we'll be there. You mentioned grilling hamburgers and hot dogs. What should I bring?"

"A side dish or dessert is always welcome."

"Rainy and I will come up with something."

"I'll look forward to it, and I'll see you Wednesday night."

19

Not long after her interview Wednesday morning, Summer texted Tony. "Job offer!!!"

He called her immediately. "Three exclamation points—you're stoked."

His chuckle coaxed out her own. "And then some. Jolynn, Renee, and I click. And the timing couldn't be better."

"When do you start?"

"They've given me ten days to review the contract and make a decision."

"You didn't accept on the spot?"

"I wanted to, but I think my attorney should look over the contract. She's always booked up, but she promised to review it by next Tuesday. We're meeting for lunch then to discuss."

"Not many could keep a cool head like that. Smart."

"Yes, I am." She laughed at herself. "Please keep this to yourself until I meet with my attorney and make my decision."

"No problem. I'll be over in a few hours."

Summer could hardly wait.

"I GOT THE FLOWERS YOU SENT," Tony's mom said when he picked her up for the Mother's Day brunch at Rosemary's that Sunday. "They're beautiful. You're so sweet." She went on her toes and kissed his cheek.

Since the tests had revealed she was cancer-free, she'd been easy to please and not as demanding, making his life easier as well. They were both happy and he wanted to keep it that way. As they headed for the CX he linked her arm through his. "Before we leave for Rosemary's, we need to have a little chat."

"Oh?" She looked worried.

He opened her door. When they were seated he laid down his cards. "With this recent medical issue, you had a legitimate reason to be scared. I was pretty concerned myself. When you're truly worried about your health, I'm here for you. But no more pretending you're sick when you aren't."

Her guilty look spoke volumes. Not wanting to hurt her feelings, he kept his tone gentle. "I know there are times when you want more attention from me. All you have to do is ask."

"I'm afraid you'll say no," she said, staring at her lap.

Oh, man. Hadn't seen that coming. Tony scrubbed his face with his hand. "I do that sometimes. I'm a busy guy. I don't mind a swift kick in the as—er, rear—from you that it's been too long. After all, you're the only mother I have."

"That I am." She gave a firm nod. "From now on, when I want to see you I'll tell you. Can we go now? I don't want to be late for our reservation."

"Someone's hungry." He started the car and backed down the driveway.

"I am, but I'm not going to overdo and I'm sticking with one cup of decaf. I don't want any trouble later. Tell me about the fishing trip."

"The guys and I had a great time and I caught a mess of fish. Better make room in your freezer for your share."

Rosemary's was swamped and service slower than usual, but at last the food arrived.

"How are the plans for the barbecue coming along?" his mother asked over the meal.

"Humming along. Nate and I need to remind businesses to deliver the gifts they promised for the raffle basket, and we're still fine-tuning the games. With the days growing warmer, we're thinking people might enjoy water activities. Sprinkler volleyball for adults and water balloon toss for the kids."

"They'll love it."

"You're welcome to come and play, too, you know."

His mother shook her head. "I'll be working that day, but I do plan to donate."

"I won't stop you."

"You'd make such a good father. I wish you had a wife and children to bring to the barbecue."

Not this again. So much for mother and son harmony. "I don't think you really want that, Ma. You find something wrong with everyone I date."

"It's not my fault you go out with people who aren't good enough for you." Tony rolled his eyes—as if that'd shut her up. "Speaking of dating, are you still seeing your mystery woman?"

He glanced at his watch. Almost ten-thirty. He needed to get out of here before they ran into Summer and her mom. He signaled for the check. "People are standing in line, waiting for a table. We should get going."

Wouldn't you know, while he waited for the bill, Summer and her party arrived.

"Look, there's Summer." His mother waved and called out to her. "Hello!"

Summer's eyes widened. She started toward then with the rest of her family in tow. "Hi, Mrs. Clark. I didn't expect to see you here. Happy Mother's Day."

"Thank you."

If his mom had any idea Summer was the woman he was involved with, he'd never hear the end of it. He nodded at Summer as if he felt nothing.

A stain flushed her cheeks. For a moment, they both avoided eye contact. Then, drawn by a magnetic force they couldn't fight, their gazes caught and held.

"It seems my daughter isn't going to introduce us," the woman beside her said. "I'm Shelley, her mother," she cooed and fluttered her lashes. "I recognize you from the firefighter calendar."

Summer seemed embarrassed, but it was no big deal. Since becoming the poster guy for the month of July, he was used to flirty women of all ages.

He flashed his teeth. "Happy Mother's Day, Shelley."

Now he knew where Summer had gotten the long legs and white-blond hair. But she was soft and sweet whereas Shelley... Her show of warmth failed to conceal her weary, hard expression, as if life had thrown her one too many curve balls. "This is my mom," he told her.

"Irene Clark." His mother's friendly look encompassed the entire group. "You must be Summer's sister and the niece and nephew I've heard about."

Shelley's eyes widened. "You heard about us?"

"Summer did my taxes until she lost her job. If I have any say, she'll be doing them again next year."

"I'd like that," Summer said. "We'll talk about it later." She introduced the rest of her family to Tony. Although he wasn't wearing his firefighter uniform, the kids were wide-eyed.

"You're coming to our barbecue and fundraiser, right?" he said. "Lots of kids will be there."

"Summer mentioned it, but I haven't decided," Rainy said.

"No pressure—show up if you feel like it." Tony took his mom's arm. "We were just leaving. Forget waiting for the bill. We'll pay up front."

"So she's your mystery woman," she commented as he drove her home.

"Why would you think that?"

"I have eyes, Tony."

Here it comes. "If you're thinking about badmouthing her, don't."

"I would never."

While he wondered at that unexpected response, she went on. "Summer is a lovely woman, smart, gorgeous, and capable of keeping you on your toes. Exactly the kind of wife I've always wanted for you. Think of the beautiful children you two—"

Tony groaned. "Leave it alone."

"All right." His mother didn't say another word but she wore a smile all the way home.

20

As the waitress showed Summer and the rest of the family to their table, Shelley nodded approvingly. "I'm impressed, Summer. A ruggedly handsome man and a local celebrity. How did you snag him?"

Tony had gotten extra sun on his fishing trip, and he did have a rugged air. But Summer wasn't about to go all hot and panting in front of her mother. "I have never in my life 'snagged' anyone. As you heard, I used to do his mother's taxes," she said, hoping her matter-of-fact tone would put an end to the speculation.

"Label it any way you want. He's smitten with you."

Oh, damn. "Help," she mouthed to Rainy, who gave a "Beats me" shrug.

"He doesn't seem your type," Shelley went on. "You usually go for the suit-and-tie type."

"Do you think we could visit the fire station sometime?" Hayden asked.

Summer wanted to kiss the boy for changing the subject.

"Can we, Aunt Summer?" Maya asked.

"Probably, but I'd call and find out. You kids must be famished, and the restaurant is extra busy today. It could take awhile to get our food. I think we should order."

The second the waitress jotted down their choices and bustled off, Shelley picked up where the conversation had left off. "You have an in with the fire station now, Summer. If you convince Tony to set up a tour for Maya and Hayden, I'd be happy to take them."

Summer just bet. "Tony is way too young for you, Mom."

"Don't you think I know that? I can be attracted to a man without chasing after him. Besides, he only has eyes for you."

"That's true," Rainy agreed.

Enough already. "Can we please drop the subject? This is supposed to be a Mother's Day brunch, not a conversation about my love life."

Shelley's eyes lit up. "I knew it! You're involved with him."

Summer nearly choked on her orange juice. That cat was definitely out of the bag. So much for keeping the relationship private.

EAGER for her attorney's assessment of the contract from Paley and Glick, Summer entered an upscale café on the south side of town. Roberta Cornish was a good twenty years older than she but they shared a drive for success in their chosen careers. Summer respected her and over the years they'd become friends of sorts. They hadn't spoken in months and spent lunch catching up.

"Since I last saw you something about you is different," Roberta commented. "I can't quite put my finger on what."

Not about to tell her attorney that she was having fantastic sex with a great guy—their friendship was based mostly on business issues—Summer shrugged. "I've been stress eating and put on a few pounds, but once I know where I'm landing, I'll take it off."

"I didn't even notice, so it's not that. There's a definite..." Roberta studied her. "For want of a better word, 'luminescence' about you. He must be pretty special."

So much for sticking to business. Summer told her the same thing she told everyone. "Tony and I aren't serious, but I enjoy being with him."

So much. He could easily become a habit. The mere thought made her nervous. She was not ready for anything long term.

Roberta nodded. "It takes time to develop a lasting relationship. Quentin and I were together seven years before we decided to get married and start a family."

"I never realized."

"We've never discussed our personal lives."

At the attorney's speculative look, Summer added, "I have no idea how long this thing between Tony and me will last, but I do know that marriage isn't on my radar right now, let alone having children."

"You're focused on your career and that's understandable. The important thing is, you're happy."

"I am. Having a job offer helps. As eager as I am to start a new chapter in my career, I can't lie that going to work for a brand-new company is a little scary."

"I felt the same way when I left the firm where I was and hung out my own shingle. I was on my own, but you'll have two partners to back you up."

"Good point. Did you have problems attracting clients?"

"At first, but I didn't let that stop me. Everywhere I went I promoted myself—parties, restaurants, even the auto mechanic's. Here I am fifteen years later, still self-employed, with two attorneys, a paralegal, and a receptionist working for me. I'm busy and happy, and I have no doubt you will be, too."

Under the table Summer crossed her fingers.

Roberta signaled the waitress to clear the meal and bring coffee, then pulled a folder from her brief-case. "Let's talk about this contract. Overall it looks good, but there are a few points to consider."

She handed Summer a copy of the document with her notes included and they set to work. Sometime later, an alarm beeped on the attorney's watch. "I have another appointment soon and need to get back to the office," she explained. "It was great to catch up."

"Thanks so much for your input." Summer shook her hand.

"Any time. Good luck with the new job and your new man."

Sitting in the car, Summer combed through Roberta's notes as well as the comments she'd added during the meeting. Then she phoned Paley and Glick. The receptionist forwarded the call to Renee.

"I just left a meeting with my attorney," she said after exchanging greetings with Renee. "There are a few details we need to iron out."

"Come on over and we'll talk."

21

L ess than an hour after meeting with Renee and Jolynn, the changes Summer requested had been initialed and three of them had signed the contract. Surely the incandescence Roberta had mentioned was twice as bright.

The two partners told her about the accountants she'd manage and set her first day of work for the following Wednesday. Elated, Summer met with the sole employee in HR, a friendly and knowledgeable professional who guided her through the usual paperwork. Having accomplished that, she exited the building with a smile she couldn't erase.

She had a job!

She texted Tony. *"Yes!"*

No reply, but the man was busy.

She couldn't reach Rainy, either, which meant her sister was also hard at work. She left a message for her to call.

Summer considered contacting Shelley, but wasn't about to tell her until her sister knew.

Too hyper to drive, she walked, no, floated around the block and made a mental list of possible new clients she wanted to recruit. Becca Chambers, the woman who'd offered her card at Sam and Adam's wedding, was at the top of the list, along with several businesses in the area.

Next, she called Dorie. They hadn't spoken or seen each other in weeks. "You're talking to the senior manager at Paley and Glick," she said.

"Congrats! You must be so relieved."

"I'm over the moon and about to pop out of my own skin!" Summer twirled around. A woman walking her dog grinned at her.

"I would be, too. Does this mean we have to cancel our vacation?"

"No way! I told the partners about that upfront. Business is so slow in mid-June, they're taking their vacations at the same time."

"Wonderful. Tell me more."

Summer shared all the details, then lowered her voice and shared her deepest fear. "They're depending on me to pull my weight and bring in clients, which we both know I'm good at. But I feel like I'm stepping off a cliff without knowing if I can fly."

"You'll not only fly, you'll soar."

Exactly what Summer needed to hear. "You're the best. Would you mind not sharing the news for the next twenty-four hours? I haven't been able to get hold of Rainy, and I want to tell her before word spreads."

"I wouldn't dream of popping your balloon. You have to tell Tony. He's been involved in this since you were laid off. Listening to you, and encouraging you..."

"I already texted him. As soon as he phones me I'll invite him over to celebrate."

"This new job, him—I approve. Who knows, he could be the one."

"Don't make more out of this than what it is," Summer warned. "We get along so well because we're not looking toward the future. That takes a lot of pressure off us both."

"You've been dating almost two months. If it were me, I'd want more of a commitment."

"I don't. It's a proven fact that my relationships with men don't last, and I refuse to set myself up for heartache."

"I don't have that kind of strength. Paul and I have barely started dating and I'm already gaga over him. Oh, he just texted. We're meeting in the lobby and going to dinner."

"Again?" Summer smiled. "How many dates is that?"

"Four, but who's counting? Let's touch base later in the week."

~

TUESDAY STARTED out hectic and stayed that way. Late in the afternoon, on the ride back to the station after rescuing a woman from a minivan seconds before the engine burst into flames, Tony checked his phone and found a text from Summer. Grinning at her message, he sent her a thumbs-up emoji and invited himself over to celebrate Wednesday night.

Double yes! she texted back.

"What does 'double yes' mean?" Nate asked, looking over his shoulder.

"Quit reading my texts."

"It's not my fault you hold your phone so anyone can see the screen. Plus, you're wearing a big grin you didn't have till you saw her text. You haven't explained the double yes."

"Not that it's any of your business, but she got a job."

"Good for her. You seeing her tomorrow night?"

"That's what the 'double' is for. We're having a celebration." Just the two of them, face to face, body to body...

"If you could see the goofball look on your face." Nate shook his head. "You more than like her—you're whipped."

Tony didn't deny it. He intended to enjoy every second with Summer for as long as it lasted.

22

"I had a crappy day and finally got the kids to bed," Rainy said when she called Summer Tuesday evening. "You sounded excited on your voice message. Tell me you have something good to say."

"I do, but how come you had a crappy day?"

"Work stuff. And—hang on." Rainy covered the phone, but thanks to her raised voice Summer heard every word. "I'm not kidding, Maya—get back in bed now!" No longer covering the phone, she sighed. "Sorry about that. I'm ready to hear about you."

"Remember the job I told you about, at the accounting firm? I got it! I start a week from tomorrow."

"Giving you seven whole days to relax. What I wouldn't give for that... Tell me about Tony. What's the latest?"

"He's coming over tomorrow night to celebrate with me."

"Awesome," Rainy said without sounding at all impressed.

Summer frowned. "You don't seem excited for me."

"Believe me, I am. I'm also jealous you have a hot guy to celebrate with."

"You'll meet someone."

"Will I?"

Rainy sounded really down. "Are you having second thoughts about breaking up with Dayton?" Summer asked.

"Not even a little. I am feeling blue, but I always get like this when it's close to that time of month. Have you told Shelley about the job?"

"I wanted you to know first. She's next on my list."

"Then I'll let you go. Love you."

As soon as her sister disconnected Summer phoned Shelley, who'd recently taken a job at a dry cleaner. "Hi, Mom. How was your day?"

"For some reason, every person in town decided to bring in their cleaning today. I had to cut both my breaks short. I'm sitting here with my feet up and a bowl of popcorn. I can hardly keep my eyes open."

"I won't keep you long," Summer said. "I have news."

"About you and Tony?"

As if she'd tell Shelley a word about that. Bad enough she'd met him at the Mother's Day brunch. "This is about work. I got a job at an accounting firm."

"That took long enough."

Not the response Summer expected. "It's a good job and in this tight market, I'm lucky to have it. Can't you be happy for me?"

"If you're happy, I'm happy. Not that I ever understood how you could possibly enjoy accounting."

Summer stifled a groan. "I'll be managing all the accountants and reporting directly to the partners. That's a big responsibility and a step up from my job at TME."

"I wouldn't want the headache, but at least you'll

be making more money." Now Shelley sounded impressed.

"Not right away—the firm is new and small—but as it grows, so will my salary. If all goes well, it won't be too long before I make partner."

"Good for you." Her mother let out a loud yawn. "I'm exhausted. I'm going to bed."

So nice to know you're proud of me. At least Tony and Dorie shared her joy. That took away the sting.

FOR YEARS, Summer had endured variations on a nightmarish dream that always featured a building. Sometimes a giant house that needed a huge amount of work. Other times, a hotel or school where she got lost in a maze of hallways and rooms, couldn't find her way out, and missed an important meeting.

Each time it happened, she woke up shaken and scared. She never knew when to expect the nightmares or what they meant, but had come to associate them with anxiety. To her relief, the dreams had become infrequent. She hadn't suffered through one since before TME had laid her off.

That changed Wednesday morning, when a particularly unpleasant version jerked her awake.

Was she that anxious about the new job? Uneasy and wanting to figure out what had triggered the dream now, she clutched her pillow and recalled the details.

A rambling, dusty house with missing floorboards, yellowing curtains, and no furniture. Lost as always, she'd searched for a way out and had stumbled on a different kind of room. Clean and bright, it drew her inside. There she found a crib and...an infant.

She had no idea what it meant or why it had oc-
curred now. Babies were the last thing on her mind.

For some reason, she remembered Rainy's comment the previous night about her period. Which led
to thinking about her own cycle. Abruptly, Summer
sat up.

Between the delicious thrill of being with Tony
and her focus on finding and securing a new job, she
hadn't given her cycle a thought. She'd never been regular, but it always happened within thirty days.

As she thought back, she was sure she hadn't had a
period in way longer than that. Maybe she was mis-
taken. She checked the pocket calendar in the drawer
of her bedside table, where she dutifully recorded the
onset of each menses. The last recorded entry had
been in early April.

Sitting up on the bed she thumbed through the
calendar. Nothing in May, and here it was, the last day
of the month.

She couldn't be pregnant. Tony always used a condom, even during the most urgent moments. Also, her
breasts were tender, a sure sign her period was about
to start.

The stress and upheaval of losing her job had
thrown her cycle off. That had to be it. Of course.

All the same, she was troubled. Which was her
nature. The infant in the dream didn't ease her anxiety any.

There was only one way to put her apprehension
to rest. As soon as she showered, dressed, and ate—
not much, as she'd lost her appetite—she drove to a
drugstore outside town, to protect her privacy, and
bought two pregnancy test kits from two different
manufacturers.

Using them was a whole other thing. The very

thought sent her into a fever pitch of nail-biting fear. Needing to talk, she called Dorie.

"For a person with a week off, you're up early," her friend said.

"I'm a wreck."

"If someone is breaking into your house, hang up and call 911!"

"Nothing like that. As far as I know, this neighborhood has never had a break-in. This is top secret, okay? I just realized my period is late. Really late."

"By how much?"

"Almost two months."

"Uh-oh." Summer pictured the wheels turning in Dorie's mind. "Did you use protection every time?"

"Always."

"I figured you did. Let's think this through. A lot has happened that could upset your system. Stress can mess up anyone's cycle, and yours has been pretty high."

"That's what I keep telling myself, but I need to find out. I just went out and bought a couple of pregnancy test kits, in case I get a false positive."

"Okay. And?"

"I'm scared to open the packages. What if I am pregnant?"

"You probably aren't."

"But what if I am?"

"Don't go there yet, Summer. Take both tests and find out."

"I need moral support. Can you come over?"

"I'm supposed to cook dinner for Paul tonight, but I'll postpone that and stop by after work."

"You won't have to if you can make it earlier. Maybe on your lunch break? Tony's coming over tonight, and I need to know before then."

"I wish I could. I'm about to head into a department meeting, then I have a conference call with the IRS about an audit for one of my clients. I can try to reschedule..."

"You don't want to do that with the IRS."

"For you, I would."

"No way. I'll be all right."

"I'm truly sorry I can't be there. Call me with the results."

"I will."

Summer bit her lip. Along with everything else in her life, she'd have to do this on her own.

23

P *lease, don't let me be pregnant.* Perched on the closed toilet seat, Summer checked the stick from the pregnancy test.

The pink plus told her what she'd feared. She was.

Don't panic. In a cold sweat, she repeated the test with the other kit. Same results.

Trembling, she called Dorie. "Both tests are positive."

"Oh, sweetie, what are you going to do?"

"I can't think right now—I'm in total shock. This explains why the waistbands of all my clothes are too tight. And I blamed stress eating."

"Sometimes pregnancies don't stick. A few weeks into my sister's first trimester she miscarried. I've heard that's fairly common the first time."

"Rainy didn't have any problems and neither did Shelley. The two things I'm certain of at this moment are that I'm pregnant and I have to tell Tony. He's going to freak out even worse than me."

"Or he could surprise you and be thrilled."

"He's no more ready for that than I am. I doubt the idea of having a baby with me ever entered his mind.

Our relationship is about the present, not the future, and the subject hasn't come up."

Dorie was silent so long, Summer frowned. "Are you still there?"

"I'm at a loss for words."

"Thanks for listening. Tell me about Paul. Seems like you're seeing a lot of him lately."

"We're getting to know each other. He's a great guy."

"Have you slept with him?"

"It's too soon."

"I wish Tony and I had started off nice and slow like you. It probably wouldn't have mattered—using protection every single time failed us. Promise me you'll get on the pill before you and Paul have sex."

"I already am."

~

WHISTLING and juggling a bottle of wine, a pizza, and Boomer's leash, Tony peered through the screen door. "Summer, are you in there? My hands are too full to open the door."

She let him in.

After putting his things down and setting his dog free, he kissed her. "Time to celebrate! Hope you're hungry, 'cause I brought a dynamite pizza from Harvey's with the works. And a bottle of wine, in case you're into alcohol again."

Instead of the enthusiastic smile he expected, Summer reacted with a somber nod. Her hair hung slipshod around her face and her shoulders slumped. Something was off.

Without giving him time to question her, she plucked up the pizza, carried it to the kitchen, and set it on the counter. Boomer received a lackluster pat before she wrung her hands.

Tony placed the wine beside the pizza and squinted at her. "You're quiet and pale. Are you sick?"

"Sit down, Tony. I need to talk to you."

A statement like that could only mean one thing—she was breaking up with him. He didn't have the words for their mind-blowing connection in and out of bed, only knew that he'd grown to need her every bit as much as food and water.

Ah hell, now he was miserable, too. Guarded, he sank onto a chair at the kitchen table and folded his arms.

Summer sat down opposite him. She clasped a thick lock of her hair between her fingers and fiddled with it. That explained the uncombed look.

"You know how excited I am about my new job," she said.

If this was about her job... "You'll be working long hours. That's cool."

"Okay." She looked puzzled. "Anyway, when I shared my good news with Rainy last night, she was in a terrible mood—cranky and depressed. She mentioned it was almost her time of the month and that she was going through her usual pre-period funk. Which got me thinking about my cycle."

That explained her mood. Relieved, he nodded. "You're about to get your period and you go through the same thing."

"Occasionally. After Rainy's comment, I realized I hadn't had mine in a while. Not that it's ever been regular, but I've never been this late."

"I have female friends who are irregular like that."

"You don't understand, Tony. I haven't had a period

since before Sam and Adam's wedding. I took a pregnancy test this afternoon. Actually, I took two."

He could guess the results from her troubled expression. Numb, he sat back. "You're pregnant."

Her unhappy nod confirmed it. "I don't understand how this could've happened. We've been so careful about using condoms."

"All it takes is one tiny leak. Maybe that first night when we were both a little drunk and sloppy."

"We'll never know for sure. We've had a lot of sex since then."

They sure had, and he'd been anticipating more tonight. Summer's startling news had upended that plan.

Pregnant. Shockwaves crashed through him. He scrubbed his hand over his face. "What do you want to do?"

Did she want to get rid of it? He didn't ask. Couldn't.

"That's a difficult question to answer. I only found out a little while ago. I need time to process."

Ditto.

"Have you ever been in this situation before?" she asked, clamping her bottom lip between her teeth.

"Never, thank God. You?"

"Of course not! I didn't plan on having a baby until I turned forty, if at all. I was on the pill until Lee and I broke up. I wish I still was."

As did Tony, but he was stuck on *if at all*. "You're not sure you want kids?"

"For good reasons. I pretty much raised Rainy and myself, and I sucked at it. I'd hate to subject a child to my mothering skills."

"Cut yourself some slack, Summer. You were a kid yourself. So you weren't perfect. No one is. You turned out fine, and from what I know of Rainy, she's doing okay."

"Have you ever known me to cut anyone, especially myself, slack?" She frowned. "I have no idea how you feel about children. Do you want them?"

"I haven't thought much about it. I sure didn't see this coming."

"You think I did? I accepted a new job yesterday. That's enough excitement for me." She gave a helpless shrug. "If I want to make a decent living and pay my bills, I need to give my all to Paley and Glick."

She looked near tears. Tony reached across the table for her hand. Her skin was ice-cold, but so was his.

"We're supposed to have an uncomplicated relationship," she said, reclaiming her hand. "This... It changes everything."

And how. He blew out a breath. "Pregnancy or not, we have to eat, and that pizza won't stay hot forever."

The corners of her lips lifted in an almost smile. "I've never been one to waste a pizza, especially from Harvey's."

He brought the box, napkins, and two plates to the table.

Her big eyes bleak with worry, Summer reached for a napkin and began to fold it.

"Look, we don't need to decide anything now," Tony reasoned. "You're barely pregnant. We have time to figure this out." He nudged the pizza her way. "Let's eat."

ummer pushed her empty plate aside. "Now that I've eaten I feel better."

"I've noticed that about you and food."

She appreciated his teasing smile. "I wish I knew what to do..."

The smile vanished. "*We*," he corrected. "I'm part of this, too."

"And every bit as conflicted. I need chocolate. When I picked up the pregnancy test kits at the drugstore, I also bought candy. Join me?"

"Sure."

Moments later, she opened the cabinet where she stored her chocolate stash, grabbed a handful of candy bars, and brought them to the table.

Tony selected one. "Do you want to watch the tube or stream a movie?"

"A movie sounds good—as long as it's a comedy."

Clutching her chocolate, Summer went into the living room and dropped to the sofa. Tony sat beside her, his arm around her shoulders. She found an old Steve Martin movie to stream.

During the opening credits Tony demolished his dessert.

As much as Summer's mouth watered to do the same, she managed only a few bites before her throat constricted.

She was pregnant, and so scared, the funny parts in the movie made her want to cry.

What was she going to do? The question ran continuously through her mind. Because no matter what Tony said about sharing the decision, she was the one carrying this baby. The final choice would be hers.

Halfway through the film, he paused the action. "I'm not into this. Are you?"

Summer shook her head. He shut the TV off, eyed her mostly uneaten candy and furrowed his brow. "It's not like you to waste chocolate."

"I can't eat it. Pathetic, huh?"

"Everything will work out." He kissed her crown, pushed to his feet, and headed for the bathroom.

While he was gone she studied the slightly rounded tummy she'd mistakenly credited to stress bingeing. Other than that, she couldn't see or feel anything different. Except for her tender breasts, which she experienced every month, she felt the same as always.

Maybe this was a false alarm and she wasn't pregnant after all.

Ha. The two tests proved otherwise.

When Tony returned he scrutinized her. "You nodded off."

"Believe me, I'm wide awake. I'm thinking."

"About what?"

"You have to ask?" As upset as she was, a yawn escaped.

"We're both wrung out emotionally. You probably want to get to bed and I need to do some thinking of my own. Unless you want me to stick around."

Ready to be alone again, she shook her head. "I'm okay."

"I'll call you tomorrow."

"It's better you don't. We both need time and space."

"Understood. I'll let myself out."

He whistled for Boomer and they left.

~

NATE WAS REPLACING his back deck, and Friday afternoon Tony headed over to help. Having at last finalized the details for the fundraiser and community barbecue a week from Saturday, they were free to focus on other stuff. Excited, Boomer tugged at his leash and pulled Tony through the gate in the backyard fence.

"About time," Nate greeted.

In the midst of tearing up the old deck, he looked dirty and sweaty and in bad need of help. Eager to lend a hand—hard physical labor would take his mind off the bombshell Summer had dropped two nights ago—Tony set Boomer free to race around the yard, then grabbed a crowbar.

"You look as bad as you do after a sleepless double shift at the firehouse." Nate grinned. "Summer must be keeping you busy at night."

Dude had no idea. Not wanting to get into that, Tony kept it short. "We're having...difficulties."

Nate gave a knowing nod. "This is about the time you and whoever you date usually do."

Nothing usual about this. Tight-lipped, Tony set to work prying up boards and tossing them at the pile Nate had started. In no time he was sweating, grunting with effort, and enjoying himself. Until a semi-rotten two-by-four broke unexpectedly and he landed on his ass.

Nate's eyebrows shot up. "You okay?"

"Except for my pride."

"We've been at it for a couple hours. It's hot out here and I'm ready to quit for the day. Will I see you at the poker game tonight?"

The crew had a standing Friday night game on a come-if-you-want basis.

Tony wiped his face with the hem of his T-shirt, then shook his head. "You?"

"I'm meeting Charlie for dinner to go over the plans for our newest client." Nate and his buddy moonlighted as designers of luxury interiors for private planes.

Tony eyed the cooler near the house. "Got any beer in there?"

"Yep, and it's nice and cold. I'll grab a couple and you open the peanuts."

Soon they were seated on the ground, shaded by a leafy oak, ice-cold beers in hand and a bag of unshelled peanuts between them.

"You should see the plane Charlie and I are working on," Nate said.

"Got any photos?"

His friend slid his phone from his pocket and showed him a few.

Tony took a long pull from the bottle. When he set it down, Nate was frowning at him.

"You hardly glanced at my photos, and you attacked my deck like a maniac. Not that I'm complaining, but this isn't like you. If I didn't know you better, I'd say you're having second thoughts about breaking things off with Summer."

Oh, man... Tony scrubbed his hand over his face. "It's not what you think."

"You two aren't splitting up?"

Tony was nowhere close to wanting that, but as Summer had pointed out, their relationship was no longer simple and carefree.

"Don't spread this around," he said. "She's pregnant."

Nate nearly choked on a peanut. "You're effin' pulling my leg. You know better than that."

"Give me some credit here. Protection isn't foolproof."

"Always works for me."

"I used to say that."

"Jeezus H. Christ. What are you and Summer going to do?"

"Hell if we know." Tony drained his beer. "I'm not ready to have a kid, but I can't handle the alternatives."

Talk about being trapped between a wall of fire and a slab of granite. Figuring out what to do had kept him tossing and turning for two long nights.

Early this morning he'd reached a decision. He tried it out on Nate. "The idea of having a baby with her is growing on me." Nate gaped at him as if he'd lost his marbles. Maybe he had. "If it has to happen now, it may as well be with Summer."

"Is that what she wants?"

"No idea."

Nate's snort filled the air. "If it were me, I'd ask her and find out. But what do I know?" He checked his watch. "It's early yet and the meeting with Charlie isn't for a couple hours. That gives us plenty of time to grab a burger or three. I could eat a whole cow."

"No thanks." Tony stood and brushed off the seat of his jeans. "I'm heading home to clean up and do some more thinking." Later he'd stop by Summer's place, take her out for gelato, and figure out the next step.

Nate nodded. "Hang in there, and see you Monday."

25

I n no shape to run into neighbors out working on their yards, Summer waited until dark to venture outside Friday evening. By then people were either in their houses or out somewhere. Sitting on the top step of her front porch, chin propped on her fist, she stared into the night and brooded over the question that had dogged her for days.

Did she want this baby? Did Tony?

She'd listed the pros and cons, had imagined the future with and without a child. With and without Tony, likely without. Sticking around wasn't his thing.

A daycare baby raised by an exhausted single mother working long hours—not ideal for raising a child. The logical answer was to get rid of the baby, but the idea sickened her. She laid a protective hand over her belly.

She spotted Tony's CX in the distance. As she watched, it slowed and turned into her driveway. She hadn't run a comb through her hair in days or put on makeup, but she couldn't worry about that now. After not speaking to a soul in two days, she was both happy for his company and apprehensive.

Moments later he strode toward her with a solemn

expression, not stopping until he reached the front steps. "I've been trying to contact you for hours."

Not even a hello?

She raised her chin. "I turned my phone off."

"Next time you do that, let a guy know. I was beginning to worry. You're okay, huh?"

"I'm freaking great," she muttered. "Where's Boomer?"

"Left him at home."

This would be a short visit, then. Summer longed for the opposite, for him to stay. But she wouldn't tell him—she didn't want to appear needy. "Shouldn't you be working on the barbecue?"

"Nothing left to do now till the day of the event. We need to talk about the future."

Afraid to meet his gaze, she picked at her thumbnail. "I'm nowhere near ready for that conversation."

"Yeah, we should probably get a gelato first."

"Gelato?" she repeated, hardly believing her ears. She'd been craving the fudge cookie sundae but hadn't been able to summon the energy to take herself. She hadn't left the house since she'd bought the pregnancy tests. The thought of running into someone she knew filled her with dread.

"I can't go tonight."

"Have something better planned?"

"Yes." It wasn't exactly a lie. She needed to do laundry and wash her hair. She also needed to figure out what to do.

"Uh-huh. That's why you're sitting out here on the front porch in the dark."

"I'm not in the mood, okay?"

"You, Summer Putnam, are turning down a chance to get your favorite ice cream, the stuff you've been talking about, for weeks."

"It's *gelato*, not ice cream, and Giordano's is a long drive from here." The flimsiest excuse ever, but she wasn't in the best frame of mind to come up with anything else.

"I promised to take you and I never renege on a promise. You know you want it."

He had no idea how bad.

His dark eyes fixed on her, making her knees weak. He offered his hand and the last remnants of her resistance dissolved. She let him pull her to her feet.

During the twenty-minute drive, Summer stared through the window. Not that she could see anything except the safety lights along the road and the headlights of occasional vehicles coming from the other direction. She glanced up, but couldn't see as many stars as she had at Tony's the night they'd made love on the chaise in his back yard. Her only concern then had been to end the evening alone in her own bed.

Had that only been a few weeks ago? It felt like a lifetime.

"That string of white lights up ahead is Giordano's," she said.

"Look at the line stretching out the door and the packed picnic tables," he commented as he eased into a parking space on the far side of the lot. "Gelato must be good stuff."

"You'll see." With nowhere to sit, people stood in groups or perched on the hoods of their cars while they ate. "I don't want to eat here."

"No problem. We'll get ours to go and take it to your house."

"I'll wait in the car while you order."

"And leave me to screw up your sundae? No way—you're coming in with me."

"If I must." Grumbling, she pulled down the sun

visor, activated the mirror light, and studied her reflection unhappily. "I'm a complete mess."

"You look okay to me."

"Ha." She ran a comb through the tangles in her hair, then applied lipstick. "That'll have to do."

To her relief, she didn't recognize anyone inside. But Tony did. He nodded and smiled at several people as they took their places at the back of the line. It seemed to be moving along.

Summer relaxed. In no time, he had the order in hand. They turned toward the exit. Outside the door, they ran into Betty Randall and several of her elderly friends on their way in.

The gray-haired gossip beamed at them. "Hello, you two. These are my friends, Betsy, Gail, and Nancy. Meet Tony Clark and Summer Putnam."

After greeting Summer, the women turned to Tony. They looked star struck. He indulged them with a broad grin that never faltered when they requested autographs. Tucking his personalized autograph in her purse, one of the women—Summer couldn't remember who was who—gestured toward the waiting customers. "We'd better get in line."

Betty nodded. "Save me a place. I'll be there shortly. Congratulations on your new job," she said, but her shrewd gaze homed in on Summer's middle.

Or so it seemed to Summer. She folded her arms across her waist and attempted to suck in her stomach. "How did you hear about that?"

"You know how fast news travels in Guff's Lake." Betty studied the cold pack in Tony's hand with interest. "My friends and I haven't been here before. What did you get?"

"A large fudge cookie sundae—Summer's favorite."

"That sounds sinfully rich."

"Not if you share." Uncomfortable under the woman's inspection, Summer tugged Tony's arm. "We need to get home before it melts."

"Enjoy every bite." Betty walked away like a woman on a mission.

"Within an hour, everyone in town will know we took our gelato to your place," Tony muttered as he headed back to her house.

"As long as they don't know the rest. Did you see her checking out my stomach? What if she knows?" Summer groaned. "We only found out a few days ago and we haven't even decided what to do."

His hooded look confused her. "We'll talk about that later," he said. "Who else have you told besides Dorie?"

"No one. Not even Rainy."

"I helped Nate with his deck this afternoon. I mentioned it, but he knows not to say anything."

"Well, someone must've blabbed."

"No point worrying about it now."

In what seemed like no time, Tony parked in her driveway. "Let's dig in before this sundae turns into a giant gelato shake."

"I'm ready." Summer plunked onto the front porch.

Tony passed her a plastic spoon from the sack and set the sundae between them. Side by side, they dug in.

"I see why this is your favorite," Tony said after a while.

Having eaten little the past two days, Summer had regained her appetite. She finished every bit of her half, then licked her spoon.

"Now we're talking." He grinned. "All better now?"

No sense pretending she was happy when she was

scared and more rattled than she'd ever been. "I'm struggling."

"I hear that."

Summer groaned. "Next Wednesday I start work. What am I supposed to tell Jolynn and Renee?"

"You don't have to say anything yet." A long silence, then, "I don't know much about pregnancy. Can I touch your belly?"

She couldn't believe he wanted to. "Go ahead, but at this stage the fetus is about the size of a blueberry. Too small for you to feel anything. I do have bigger stomach than I'm used to. That's what Betty was staring at."

"I don't see that."

She leaned back a fraction. Tony placed his big, warm hand on her belly so tenderly, she wanted to cry. Darn her hormones making her super emotional.

"You're right—what I feel is all you," he said.

Wouldn't you know, at that very moment Selena drove past and honked. Pasting a smile on her face, Summer straightened and waved. "I can picture her leering expression. I can't face her right now."

"I could use a glass of water. Let's go inside."

In the kitchen, Tony gulped his water, then spun to face her. "We have a lot to talk about and decisions to make."

"I told you I'm not ready."

"Still, I need to speak my piece." He gestured at the table. "Sit."

Did he want the baby? What would he say? Trembling inside, Summer took a seat.

~

"THIS BABY THING... You're not the only one who had a rough few days," Tony admitted as he joined Summer at the table. "We have to look toward the future."

She raised her chin as if shoring herself up. For what? He'd find out soon enough. He cleared his throat. "I'll cut right to the point. I want this baby."

If not for the slight widening of her eyes, he'd have thought she'd shut down. He couldn't read her at all. "Tell me you want the same thing," he said, unable to mask the pleading tone of his voice.

At last, a reaction. She hugged herself and let out a weighty sigh. "I couldn't live with any other option."

Thank God. He sagged in relief. She seemed more resigned than thrilled, but that wasn't hard to understand. Adjusting to something this huge and unexpected took time. What most mattered was they agreed about the baby.

One decision down, a thousand to go.

"If Betty has heard about the pregnancy, she'll spread the word like wildfire," Summer said. "We ought to tell our families before someone else does, but ugh—I'm not ready for that." She recoiled. "I can't imagine Rainy's reaction, and God knows what my mother will say. Or yours."

Like Summer, Tony wasn't ready to face his mother. "She likes you and claims she wants grandkids, but I can't deal with her yet. Let's assume Betty doesn't know and keep this to ourselves a few more days."

"Okay. Their finding out is the least of our worries."

She had that right. "We're in this together and we'll get through it." He reached for her hand, but she didn't take it.

"The pregnancy is only the beginning, Tony. What happens after the birth?" She ducked her head and rapped her forehead with her knuckles. "Renee and Jolynn will think I tricked them into hiring me."

"Tell them the truth, that you didn't know. They're smart women—they'll be cool with it."

"Until I give birth and take maternity leave. They expect to give my all to the job."

"And you will. A baby won't change your commitment to the company or your career. We'll take care of our baby together. Let's call her 'her' for now."

He pictured a mini-Summer running around with a pros and cons list and smiled to himself. "I only work Mondays and Tuesdays, and the tree business takes at most a couple hours a week. The rest of the time I'm available."

"Newborns are hard work. They require constant attention, day and night. When Rainy had Hayden, she was still living with his father. Even with his support they were both sleep-deprived and overwhelmed. A few months in, the responsibility became too much for him."

"But eventually he adjusted, right?" Tony guessed.

Summer shook her head. "He walked away."

"From his own kid? Real nice guy. I'm trained to deal with tough situations," Tony assured her. "Lack of sleep doesn't bother me, either. I'm a firefighter—I'm used to getting by on two to three hours' rest."

"Twice a week, but this is a 24/7 job with no days off. Anyway, you're not the one who'll be doing the breastfeeding."

"I can do everything else. Especially if we move in together." An offer he'd never made to any woman, but these were special circumstances. Plus, living with Summer, coming home to her and their baby after his shift, appealed to him.

Which showed how bat shit crazy he was for her. Yep, he had it bad.

She pushed her hair behind her ears. "Ignoring the fact that neither of us is anywhere close to wanting to live together, your plan won't work. Like every other man in my life, you're bound to grow tired of me."

Say what? "I'm nothing like Rainy's ex or yours, or any of the jerks who've let you down," he said, wanting to knock their idiot heads together. "You're smart, beautiful, and fun to be with. Only a fool would give you up."

"You don't want any complications, remember?"

"You're carrying my baby. That's a complication I can get on board with. And FYI, I'm not tired of you, not by a long shot. When we're apart you're all I think about. When we're together I can't get enough of you. It's never been like this for me."

"You're talking about sex. You know how much I enjoy making love with you, but we can't survive on that alone. We don't love each other."

"We sure like each other a lot, and we'll both love our kid."

"We are not living together." She compressed her lips.

"Okay, for now we won't, but after she's born—"

"I can't commit to that, and neither should you. Who knows how we'll feel in five or six months?"

"At least keep the option on the table. If you haven't changed your mind when the baby is born, we'll live apart. We can still both raise her."

"Like a joint custody thing? At the moment that sounds good, but what if you meet someone, say two years from now, and fall in love? What if I do? What happens then?"

The thought of Summer loving another man made

Tony furious, but if he wanted to press his point he couldn't afford to get sidetracked. "This is my kid we're talking about, Summer. I'm in for the long haul."

"You'd better be. I grew up without a father and it left a big hole in me. If our child had to suffer through that... I swear, I'd kill you."

Her fierce, protective look only made him more determined to win her over.

"Don't forget, I lost my dad, too. Sure, I had seventeen years with him—when he was around—but he still left. You think I want that for our kid?"

As determined and sincere as he was, Summer didn't seem convinced. "I feel like we're going around in circles, and I'm tired of talking. I haven't slept much in days, and I need to get to bed. It'd be nice to start work next week with energy and enthusiasm. Oh, God, I have to tell Jolynn and Renee."

"Don't make this worse than it needs to be by stressing about that. Get some rest, and promise me you'll think about what we discussed."

She nodded. He left her sitting at the kitchen table, staring at her hands.

26

On the first day of Summer's new job, she wore a lightweight blazer to hide the unbuttoned placket of her too-snug skirt. At some point she'd have to switch to maternity clothes. Excited to start work and also anxious at the thought of revealing her pregnancy to Renee and Jolynn, she showed up early to tell them.

"Good morning," Jolynn greeted her with a wide smile. "We don't serve doughnuts often, but this is a special occasion. With the bulk of tax season behind us, some of the staff are out on vacation. The rest will arrive around nine. Once everyone is here, we'll introduce you."

Summer bit back a bad case of nerves. "If possible, I'd like to meet with you and Renee right away."

"Of course. Renee is on the phone with a client, but she shouldn't be long. While we wait, let's get something to drink."

In the lunch room, a clean, smallish space with the usual refrigerator, tables, and microwave, Jolynn gestured at the coffeemaker. "It's fresh. We also have tea."

Having drunk coffee on the drive to the office and not wanting to overdo the caffeine now that she was expecting, Summer made herself an herbal tea. By the time she and Jolynn had their mugs in hand and sat down at a table, Renee had joined them.

"Welcome," she said, her greeting as warm as Jolynn's. She refilled her coffee and joined them.

"Don't be nervous—we're all friendly here," Jolynn teased.

Realizing she was fussing with her mug to get it centered in front of her, Summer folded her twitchy fingers over her stomach. "I'm thrilled to be here," she said. "But I think you should know... Not long after we signed the contract I had an unsettling dream and I remembered..." Not wanting to bore them with unnecessary details, she plunged ahead. "What I'm trying to say is, I'm pregnant."

Jolynn and Renee looked surprised.

"I don't want you thinking I knew when I interviewed for this job, because I didn't," Summer added. "If I had, I'd have told you. This came as a huge shock to both me and the man I'm seeing."

"You're still going to work here, though," Jolynn said.

"Absolutely, and I want to assure you, I won't let the pregnancy or the baby interfere with my job."

"Renee and I both have children, and we're well aware that there are times when their needs come first. Especially when they're little. Mine are in middle school, but I remember what life was like when they were small."

"I have a two-year-old." Renee shook her head. "He can be a real challenge, but that comes with the territory. What's your due date?"

"I haven't seen a doctor yet, but I'm about two months along."

"January, then."

"Right at the start of tax season. Terrible planning, I know. Only this wasn't planned at all." To Summer's horror, her eyes filled. If only she wasn't so emotional. She blinked hard.

Jolynn handed her a tissue box. "We'll work around that."

Renee nodded. "There are a couple of great day-cares nearby, one that accepts infants. You'll want to get on the list for that today. I'll get you the information this morning."

Relieved, Summer dabbed her eyes. "Thank you both for understanding."

Jolynn checked her watch. "By now, everyone should be here. Shall we go into the conference room and introduce you?"

~

SUMMER WAS FINISHING dinner when Tony called. "How did your first day go?"

"Really well." More relaxed than she'd been in ages, she smiled. "You were right, Jolynn and Renee took my pregnancy in stride. I'm ready to tell Rainy."

"I'm almost there myself. I'm planning to share the news with my crewmates at the Friday night poker game. I wouldn't want to spring something like that on them at the community barbecue Saturday."

"Okay, but what about your mother?"

"She invited me to dinner Sunday. I'll tell her then."

"I'll probably phone Shelley tonight, after my call to Rainy." Summer groaned. "I dread that. All the questions... Most of which we haven't answered ourselves."

"They'll have to deal with that. Are your sister and her kids still coming Saturday?"

"As far as I know."

"The festivities begin at eleven. Some of the activities involve water play, so wear clothes you don't mind getting wet, and let them know."

Imagining what she'd look like in a shirt clinging to her belly, which seemed to grow by the week, and the gossip sure to follow, Summer swallowed. "I'm not sure I'll make it."

"Why not? I want you there."

"Facing your firefighter crewmates and their girlfriends and wives... That's going to be hard."

"How so?"

"You're really asking?"

"They're good people—they'll take their cues from us. If we're happy, they'll be happy."

"They'll judge me."

"For Pete's sake, it's not as if we robbed a bank. We're having a baby."

"Yes, I know."

"You're ashamed."

"No!" She paused to think about that. "In a way, I guess I am. I've always prided myself on being prepared. I don't like surprises, and this pregnancy... I'm still adjusting to the idea."

"You can't plan everything in your life, Summer. Stuff happens and when it does, you roll with it and forge ahead. Like you did when your former company laid you off."

"Yes, but I had no control over that."

"You didn't have control over the failure of the protection we used, either."

She bit back tears. Second time today. Get a grip.

"Summer, are you there?"

She sniffled. "Yes."

"You're crying."

"No, I'm not."

"I can hear you. You're bawling your eyes out."

"It's the pregnancy," she wailed, giving up the pretense of emotional control. "I'm all hormonal."

"Sounds as if you could use a hug. I can be there in fifteen minutes."

A hug wouldn't fix the problem, and she wasn't up to seeing Tony. She blew her nose. "I'm okay now. I have to get up early tomorrow and I still want to make those calls."

"Tell me I'll see you Saturday."

"You will," she said, but she was uneasy about it.

This whole baby thing made her want to crawl under the covers and stay there. Unfortunately, that wasn't possible. Anyway, she was no coward.

She cleaned up her dinner mess and pulled herself together. Then she phoned her sister.

27

Rainy answered on the second ring. "Hey, big sister."

"You sound relaxed. Hayden and Maya must be in bed."

"They are, and for some lucky reason they both settled right down. I'm sprawled on the sofa, sipping a glass of wine and getting ready to watch a show. I gather you survived your first day at the new job."

"I enjoyed it. I have news."

"Hold on while I turn off the tube. Okay, I'm all ears. I'll bet this is about you and Tony. Let me guess—you're moving in together."

"You know me better than that. I've never lived with a man."

"I know, I know, you're an independent woman. I wish I was more like you. If you're not moving in to-gether... Wait—did he propose?"

For the first time all day, Summer laughed. Okay, not a genuine laugh, but close. "You're way off." Starting with her unsettling dream, she caught her sister up. "This has totally blindsided both Tony and me," she finished.

"There must be something wrong with my ears. I

thought you said something about a pregnancy? You, Miss Perfect, who preplans every detail of your life? I have to admit, I'm stunned."

"I'm hardly perfect. I've made my share of mistakes. I totally misjudged Lee. Now this baby..." Summer cupped her belly, which over the past few days had somehow become standard practice.

"Pregnancy happens, and don't I know it. We've both had rotten luck with men. But professionally? You put yourself through college, passed your CPA exam on the first try, and found a dream job. Now you've found an even better one. All because you mapped out your career and followed that map every step of the way."

"I don't have any complaints about that. My new bosses have been one hundred percent supportive and understanding about my little surprise."

"They'd better be. If you think back, you'll remember that I wasn't thrilled about either of my pregnancies, but I'm awful glad to have Hayden and Maya. You'll see, things will work out."

"That's what Tony says."

"He seems like a good guy."

"He claims he wants this baby, but you and I both know that his feelings today are no guarantee of his feelings tomorrow." Summer didn't for one minute trust that he'd stick around. He intended to be part of their child's life—that she believed. But he wouldn't stay with her.

Rainy sighed. "There is that. Whatever happens, I'm here for you and I'll help any way I can."

Despite her worries, Summer brightened. "Have I told you lately that you're the best sister ever?"

"I try. I can't wait to tell Hayden and Maya about their new cousin. When are you calling Shelley?"

"As soon as we hang up. I'll let you know how that goes when I pick you up Saturday."

~

EARLY SATURDAY MORNING TONY, Nate, and the rest of the crew met at Orchard Park to set up for the community event. The city had contributed the park and a large tent. The rest was up to the GLFD.

Mother Nature had cooperated fully, with a cloudless sky and little wind—perfect weather for drawing a big crowd. With any luck, the day would pass without a hitch, but erring on the cautious side, Max had parked one of the aid cars near the park entrance.

When they finished the job, large, folding tables for the expected side dishes lined the tent, along with plates, cups, and cutlery. Fuel and coolers filled with long-lasting ice packs and hamburger patties and hot dogs sat at the ready beside the park's giant barbecue grills. Designated areas for regular games and those involving water play had been marked off, and banners announcing the event had been hung in strategic places.

Tony checked his watch. "Forty minutes and counting," he announced, and Nate gathered everyone together. "You all know your assignments. Nate and I will be walking around, making sure everything runs smoothly. If you need something from us, holler. Questions?"

Only Captain Comings spoke up. "I didn't get an assignment."

"As captain, your job is to look pretty."

"I can do that." He struck a vain pose.

When the laughter died down, Nate chimed in. "Our goal today is to raise money for new equipment and show the community what good guys we are. Let's do this!"

Woots and whistles followed. The men started to disband, but the captain signaled for them to come back. Then he nodded at Tony. "I understand congratulations are in order."

Since last night's poker game, word of Summer's pregnancy had spread. At first his teammates had been subdued, but as he'd expected their attitudes had changed when he told them he looked forward to being a father.

First to arrive were the captain's wife and three kids. Then Sam and her son, William, along with the girlfriends of other crewmates. Tony pictured Summer and their baby arriving with this group next year and grinned.

Even before the eleven o'clock opening people began showing up. Families, singles, kids—young, old, and in-between. After that, Tony was too busy to do more than periodic checks on the crew and the crowd. He kept an eye out for Summer and her sister and kids.

The fire department expected three hundred to four hundred people, and by the size of the crowd their estimate was dead-on. In short order, side dishes filled the food tables in the tent and the smell of sizzling barbecue wafted through the air. People staked out picnic tables and grassy areas for eating and relaxing.

"Big turnout," Nate commented at some point.

Tony nodded. He looked at his watch again. Almost noon and time to officially welcome everyone. Still no sign of Summer. Where was she?

28

R ainy texted she was running behind schedule and asked Summer to pick her and the kids up thirty minutes late. Her niece and nephew had barely buckled into the back seat when they bombarded her with questions about their cousin-to-be.

"Is it a boy or a girl?" Hayden asked.

Summer glanced at him in the rearview mirror. "I have no idea."

"What are you going to name the baby?" Maya asked.

"I don't know that, either. What I do know is, he or she will be lucky to have such great cousins."

Beaming and satisfied for the moment, the two settled down and amused themselves with kid-style electronic devices.

Rainy turned on the radio so the kids couldn't hear. "What did Shelley say?"

"You know how she is. It's all about her. She's already put her foot down about babysitting."

"She said the same thing to me, but once the babies came she changed her tune—as long as she doesn't have to watch them often or for more than an hour. She didn't say anything about Tony?"

"That with his looks and mine the baby will be beautiful. She doesn't expect him to stick around, either." Summer glanced at her sister. "Are you sure you want to go to this barbecue? We could have lunch someplace, then see a matinee..."

"You're joking. The kids and I have been looking forward to this all week. Water play in this heat—we'd be crazy to miss that. Plus, all those gorgeous firefighters in one place... Maybe I'll get lucky like you did, and—" She frowned at Summer. "You don't want to go."

Summer didn't hold back. "I'm not excited, no. The last time Tony and I talked... We left so many things unsettled. I'm not sure what to expect."

"You had a fight?"

"I wouldn't go that far. He wants this baby and I'm getting there. But we have different views on what should happen now and later."

Her sister dismissed the concerns with a wave. "You're only a couple of months along. You have plenty of time to work out the details. If you're like me, you'll figure stuff out as you go."

"In other words, wing it? That's not my style, and you know it."

After a quick glance at the back seat, Rainy lowered her voice. "If you don't want to lose your mind, you'd best loosen up when the baby arrives."

"Giving into chaos is no way to live. Don't tell me you've forgotten what our childhood was like."

"Oh, I remember. I also know from experience that I can guide and teach my kids, but forcing them into a box doesn't work any more than trying to make a man love you. There's the park, and look at all those people. I doubt we'll find a parking place around here."

Summer avoided the lot in the park. After a fruitless search on the adjacent streets, she gave up and found a spot a few blocks away.

As they exited the car and sauntered toward the event, Rainy placed her hands on both children's shoulders. "We're going to have so much fun."

She gave Summer a *Got that?* look.

Dreading the afternoon ahead, Summer grumbled but gave in. "I'll try."

Toting a picnic blanket and a sack of bakery cookies, Summer and her family took their places in the line to enter the park.

"Everyone in town must be here," Rainy commented.

"Not quite, but Tony expects several hundred."

After paying the entrance fee, Summer and her sister bought raffle tickets from Owen and Hank. Rainy flirted outrageously, but aside from friendly smiles, neither of the handsome firefighters bit.

"Congratulations on the pregnancy," Owen told Summer.

Hank nodded. "Pretty cool news."

They would comment on that first thing. "Thanks."

As they pocketed their tickets and joined the throng Rainy was almost salivating. "Did you see those two hunks of burning love?"

"They both have girlfriends."

"Shoot me now! I don't know where we'll find a place to put our stuff. Hey, there's Tony, over by the tent."

Holding a microphone, he stood near a "Food" banner tacked to the front. "Welcome, everyone," he said. "Guff's Lake firefighters love our community, and we look forward to having fun and giving you a chance to get to know us. Don't hesitate to introduce yourself.

"Those three guys over there—" He nodded at Rafe, Gus, and Max, who waved—"are giving tours and demos at the station. You can check out one of our fire trucks and aid cars. And don't forget our raffle. The money we raise will help us buy a new thermal imaging camera and a jaws of life, equipment we use to save lives."

He held up an enormous wicker basket wrapped in transparent cellophane. "The winning ticket takes home this basket loaded with treats, discount coupons, and giveaways donated by local businesses. Great stuff like discounts on river rafting and camp-sites, coffee, wine, restaurant meals, Samantha's Treats, and Tommie's Hair and Nails. Also a half-price coupon for a weekend at the Guff's Lake Resort hotel, and lots more.

"We have games for kids and grownups, including water balloon tosses and sprinkler volleyball. You don't want to miss those."

He was so comfortable talking to the group, so en-thusiastic, charismatic, and handsome, that almost everyone dug into their wallets for a chance at win-ning the basket.

Having never been able to relax in front of a crowd of virtual strangers, Summer envied his poise. Her heart swelled with admiration, along with other emo-tions she wasn't ready for. Feelings that went far deeper than simply liking Tony and enjoying his company.

She was falling in love with him. That scared her more than the pregnancy.

Love had never been part of the equation for her and Tony. The reason their relationship worked so well was a mutual agreement to avoid serious emotions.

Tony didn't love her. She didn't expect him to. He didn't want love from her, either, which suited Summer fine—she was far from ready to trust him with her heart. Because when he grew tired of her... Her body and soul shared collective shudders.

She couldn't, would *not* allow herself to love him.

Suddenly he saw her. He nodded, his eyes lit with warmth, and bam! Her rebel heart thudded so hard, she was sure others nearby heard its lovesick drumming.

Forget not falling for him. She already had.

Her hand went protectively to her belly. "I really screwed up and I have no idea what to do," she murmured to the embryo inside her.

Rainy gave her a funny look. "What did you say?"

Not ready to confide in anyone, especially in such a public place, Summer put her finger over her lips. "I'm trying to listen."

"Today's barbecue is on us," Tony was saying. "Thanks for bringing a lot of great-looking side dishes. Eat hearty and above all, have fun!" He turned off the mic and started toward her.

She couldn't face him until she corralled her feelings. Squinting through her sunglasses, she scanned the grounds. "I see a shady place to sit on the far side of the picnic tables. We'd better hurry before someone else grabs it."

29

I n the middle of Tony's welcome speech, he homed in on a woman in a blue baseball cap and sunglasses. Summer had finally shown up. The tension in his shoulders and gut eased considerably.

She looked cute in that hat. As soon as he finished his welcome he headed straight for her—or tried. Half a dozen people waylaid him, talking, asking questions, and wanting to schedule tours. Two women asked him to give them a call, each handing him a scribbled phone number. He crumpled both and deposited them in the nearest trash.

He lost her in the crowd, then thanks to that blue hat, located her again, standing under one of the oak trees near the picnic tables. As he drew closer, she spread a blanket on the ground. Hayden and Maya waved and greeted him with big smiles. He grinned. "Good to see you two. Lots of kids here today."

Hayden nodded and looked longingly at a group of boys horsing around nearby.

"Why don't you go over there and play with them?" Rainy asked.

The boy shrugged and ducked his head. He was at that awkward age when joining in was no longer effortless. Taking a cue from him, his sister stayed at his side.

Having spoken at a number of schools, Tony knew a thing or two about getting kids involved. "We're about to start our sack race."

"What's a sack race?" Maya asked.

"A game, and there are prizes. You can find out how to play over there." He gestured at the games area. "All kids are welcome. The race starts in five minutes."

Hayden brightened. "Come on, Maya!"

As they pivoted away to leave, Rainy called after them. "Have fun, and when you're ready for lunch, Summer and I will be right here."

They ran off. Tony nodded at Summer's sister. "Good to see you again."

"You, too. You were great with Hayden. He's shy, but you knew what to say to encourage him. You're a natural with kids, and you're going to make a great father. Congrats."

"Thanks." He pulled Summer over and flipped up her shades for a quick kiss. "It took me awhile to get over here."

"You're busy."

"You can say that again. The captain and the rest of the crew know about the baby."

"Owen and Hank congratulated me when I came in, and with the thumbs-up I've been getting from everyone, I figured as much."

She wouldn't meet his eyes. What was that about?

"I should put these cookies in the food tent." Rainy slipped away, leaving him alone with Summer.

"How're you doing?" he asked.

"I'm a little queasy today, but I'm pregnant. I'm going to make appointment with an OB soon."

"Great. When you do, let me know and I'll come with—"

"Yo, Tony!" Owen called out. "Need you over here."

Tony signaled he'd be a minute, then shrugged at Summer. "Gotta go, but I'll be back in time for lunch. Save me a place."

When he returned with his food sometime later, Summer was sitting cross-legged on the blanket with her sister and several of his crewmates' girlfriends. No sign of the kids, which meant they were off playing. Food filled Summer's plate, but unlike everyone around her, she wasn't eating.

"Tony's a—" Sam was saying. Noticing him, she cut herself off and scooted over, making a space for him beside Summer.

"I'm a what?" He raised his eyebrows and put his arm around his woman.

He felt her tremble, and not in a good way. That and her lack of appetite worried him. He ran his eyes over her. "Is your stomach still bothering you?" he murmured for her ears only.

"It's nothing." She smiled, then popped a piece of cornbread into her mouth, neither of which reassured him. He couldn't shake the feeling that something was wrong.

"I was about to toot your horn," Sam said in answer to his question. "You and Nate put together a terrific event. You've drawn quite a crowd and they're keeping you busy—all of you." Her gaze rested on Adam.

"Don't expect that to change until this thing ends at three o'clock and we clean up the mess."

Hungry, Tony dug in. He managed to put a decent dent in his meal before the captain called him over.

"See what I mean?" he said. "Water balloon fights for the kids and sprinkler volleyball for adults start soon. Enjoy." He kissed Summer and stood. "I'll see you later."

~

AFTER LUNCH SUMMER played sprinkler volleyball in her cutoffs and tee, which was great fun and helped keep her cool on the hot afternoon—on the outside. Inside she was a mess of conflicting emotions. She was grateful that Tony's hectic duties kept him occupied and away from her, a necessity until she figured out how to deal with her feelings and protect herself.

Little late for that.

Maya and Hayden got a good drenching from the water balloon game, then trotted back to the picnic spot, delighted with themselves but worn out from the activities and excitement.

They weren't the only ones. Hiding such strong feelings was a ton of work. If that wasn't enough, Summer's stomach had decided to do somersaults. "We've had enough fun in the sun and I'm not feeling so good," she told Rainy.

Her sister gave her a sympathetic look. "At times, pregnancy can be a bitch. Anyway, it's almost three o'clock and the festivities are winding down. We'll leave as soon as you say good-bye to Tony."

"I would if I knew where he went." Her preference was to avoid him, but she wasn't going to be rude about it.

"I'll pack up and you go look for him."

Summer heaved a giant sigh, part fatigue and part dread.

"Poor you," Rainy said, all concerned. "I'll find him. Hayden and Maya, gather our things and wait here with Aunt Summer."

Within minutes, Rainy returned with Tony. "Toss me your keys," she told Summer. "The kids and I will pick you up at the entrance—give us ten minutes. Thanks, Tony. We had a super time."

"Great to see you."

He found an empty chair. Summer sank into it and he hunkered down next to her. In full paramedic mode, he checked her pulse and studied her with a critical eye. "Your color is good and your pulse rate is normal. Are you still feeling queasy?"

"A little."

"It's hot out here." He adjusted her hat to better shade her eyes, so gentle and caring she wanted to cry.

"Tell me what's bothering you," he said. "I'll bet I can help."

I'm in love with you. Nothing he could do to fix that. Afraid her expression would betray her, she picked at a thread on the hem of her cutoffs. "I don't—I can't talk about it."

"You're upset with me. I wanted to spend more time with you, but it's been crazy."

"That's not it at all. This isn't about you."

His eyes narrowed. "That sounds like the beginning of a classic breakup line."

He pushed to his feet and Summer bit her lip. "I just... I need..." What did she need?

To her surprise, a voice in her head answered loud and clear. Better to tell him the truth now than hold it in and make herself sicker. Because face it, controlling her feelings was impossible. She'd probably regret this later, but she needed to get them out.

Even the thought of telling him eased her roiling stomach. "Okay, okay," she mumbled, mustering her courage.

Hating Tony's guarded look, she squared her shoulders. "Can we go someplace more private?"

He glanced around, then gave her a hand up. Moments later they slipped between a big tree and the tall bushes on the back side of the Welcome to Orchard Park sign, away from prying eyes.

Standing a surprising distance from her given the enclosed space, he stiffened as if bracing himself. "Tell it to me straight."

All kinds of nerves clamored inside her and she almost lost her resolve. But not quite. She cleared her very dry throat. "Something in me changed today, and I realiz—"

"Tony, where you at?" someone called out.

His eyes never left her. "Go on."

"Shouldn't you go help that person?"

"They'll keep." He shoved his hands in his pockets and widened his stance. "Well?"

"My feelings for you..."

She broke off as the clamor inside filled her head and grew deafening. Dizziness flooded her and her vision clouded.

Then everything went dark.

30

Summer had fainted. Reacting at lightning speed, he caught hold of her, but not before the back of her head smacked into the tree. Hard enough to scare him. "Summer, can you hear me?"

Out cold. His heart in his throat, he shouted over the noise. "SOS!"

No place to lie her down where they were. Mindful of her injury, he carried her out and laid her on the grass.

Max was closest and the first to arrive, then the rest of the crew. A mass of people began to form around them. Several crewmates secured a safety perimeter while Tony examined her, starting with the ugly bloody gash on the back of her head.

"I need a dressing," he ordered.

Someone handed the sterile supplies and a neck brace to Max. As Tony put the brace in place, securing Summer's head and neck, she began to stir. He sucked in his first full breath since she'd passed out. "She's coming to."

Groaning, Summer regained consciousness. "What are you doing? My head hurts."

Tony held her down. "Stay still, Summer. You fainted."

She complied. "I don't remember that. You put something around my neck."

"Just in case. Now I'm going to patch up your head."

"I'm bleeding?"

"Yep. You banged into a tree pretty hard." Tony applied and secured the bandage.

"Why did I pass out?"

For any number of reasons, many of them alarming. If anything happened to her or the baby... A lump formed in his throat. "Could be the heat—I'm not sure." He raised her eyelids and peered at her eyes. "One pupil is larger than the other. You have a concussion. We're going to the ER."

Max brought over a hand gurney. Together, he and Tony lifted her onto it. Tony strapped her in, and they started toward the aid car in the parking lot.

"What about Rainy and the kids?" she asked, still sounding woozy.

"If they're waiting for you at the park entrance, we'll meet them on the way to the aid car. If not, one of the crew will let them know where you are." He nodded at Nate, who'd been handling crowd control. "Can you finish up here without me?"

"You bet. Keep us informed."

31

After leaving Summer in the exam room with her sister, the kids, and Dr. Hoyt, an ER doc Tony knew and trusted, he waited in the lounge area with Max.

Knowing she was in good hands eased some of his worries. But not all of them. "Summer wants to break up with me," he said.

His crewmate's jaw dropped. "I don't think so. Have you seen her face when she looks at you? Believe me, she wants to keep you around."

"That's what I thought, but she said something had changed and gave me the 'It's not you' line. Before she could explain herself, she passed out."

"You don't know for sure what she was going to say."

"Are you kidding? That's my line, and I know what it means." Tony scrubbed his hand over his face. "Hearing it from Summer sucks."

"Big time. Are you in love with her?"

Tony wasn't sure, but his mouth was. "Hell, yes."

A huge thing to admit even to himself, but there it was.

He loved her. He shook his head in wonder. "I

don't want to lose her, man. I need to tell her right away, before she breaks up with me."

He strode toward the ER exam rooms. She was in a room at the end of the hall, sitting on the exam table, getting a fresh bandage on the back of her head and talking with Dr. Hoyt. Crammed into the space on the other side of the table, Rainy and her kids listened.

Emotions clogged Tony's throat. Fighting for control, he hesitated in the threshold before he went in. "Hey," he said, his voice on the verge of cracking.

"Hi." Her soft smile lit him up inside.

"How's your head?"

"Four stitches. They had to shave the area around it." She made a face.

"It'll grow back. Everything okay with Summer and the baby?" he asked, his eyes on Dr. Hoyt.

"Other than the concussion, both are fine," the doc replied.

Summer looked sheepish. "I fainted because I was dehydrated."

Screw control. Tony teared up in relief. "Thank God that's all it was." He shook his head at her. "From now on, you're going to drink a lot more water."

Her nod was unusually meek.

"She's already started," Dr. Hoyt said, nodding at the near-empty pitcher on the hospital table. "You're free to go, Summer, but someone should keep an eye on you for the next day or two."

The doctor left and Tony took his place. "I'll do that."

"Would you?" Rainy beamed at him. "My apartment is so little, I don't have the room. Summer doesn't have space for the three of us, either." She turned to Summer. "I'll drive your car to my house and keep it there until you're able to pick it up."

"Okay with you?" he asked Summer. "Wait—before you answer that, I need to talk to you. Alone."

When her family cleared out, he shut the door, nudged her over, and sat down beside her on the exam table. "Before you fainted, you were about to break up with me." She opened her mouth, but he placed his finger against her lips. "Let me plead my case. Between my knowing you wanted to end things and you passing out, you scared the crap out of me. Maybe that's what it took to get the truth through my thick skull."

Fighting for the woman he loved, he held nothing back. "I'm crazy about you, Summer. I love the way you come apart when I touch you, and every claw mark you put on my back. I love your fierce independence, your strength, and the way you fight for what you want. Your sweet tooth is as bad as mine, and when your stomach is empty, you pack away almost as much as I do. You don't nag me or try to manipulate me.

"Hell, I don't even mind your pros and cons lists. And I already love our baby. So no, your decision to break up with me is unacceptable." She opened her mouth again, but he cut her off. "I'm not done. We have a great thing going, the best relationship I've ever had. I can't force you to stay with me, but I won't give up trying. Now I'm finished."

"Good, because I have things of my own to say." She put her hands on her hips. "Silly man, I never wanted to break up. I realized I'd fallen in love with you and I got scared, so I backed away. Then—"

"Hold on. You love me?"

"Very much."

His heart ballooned in his chest. "Why didn't you tell me and save us both a lot of grief?"

"Because we agreed that love wasn't part of our relationship—that and my dismal history with men. I was afraid if you knew my true feelings, you'd walk away. I made a decision to tell you anyway, but then I fainted."

He cupped her chin. "You have big trust issues, know that?"

"And you don't?"

"My issues have to do with manipulative women who'd rather play me than tell me straight what they want. Your straightforwardness is one reason I fell for you. I trust you completely." He kissed the tip of her nose. "If we're going to have a future together, you have to trust me."

Her eyes widened. "You want a future together."

"That's right."

They drank in the sight of each other, two parched lovers on the verge of quenching their thirst. Mindful of her concussion, he pulled her into a tender kiss that ended far too soon.

She snuggled up close and he never wanted to let her go.

"Why don't you stay at my place tonight," he said. "I'll cook for you and spoil you rotten. I plan to do a lot of that. For the rest of our lives, if you'll have me."

"If I'll... Did you just propose?"

He hadn't planned to, but now that he had, he was totally on board. "In my clumsy way, I did. But even if you don't want to get married or live together I'm in for good, no matter what. Are you with me? If you need to make a list of pros and cons before you answer, I'll wait."

"I don't need a list for this." She crooked her finger at him, then kissed him. "I'm not quite ready to move in together, but yes, I am so with you."

His chest expanded with emotions. "Don't ever lose that independent streak, Summer. As long as I know you love me, I'm cool with whatever you decide. Damn, I love you." Another kiss, then he smiled at her. "What are your thoughts on us getting married?"

"I like the idea. In two weeks, Dorie and I are leaving for our vacation, but let's set a date after I get back."

"You mean that?" She nodded and he pumped his fist. "All right!"

He was going in for another kiss when a firm knock sounded at the door. Nate poked his head in, then opened the door wide. A bunch of the crew stood behind him. "Everything okay?"

Tony flashed a smile. "Yeah. What are you doing here?"

"Checking in. We cleared enough money to buy both the jaws of life and the thermal camera."

"That's good news."

Ethan elbowed Nate aside. "We're awful glad you're okay, Summer."

"Me too," she said. "You guys are the best."

Suddenly her cell phone rang. So did Tony's.

"That's Shelley," she said.

"My mom, too."

Rainy squeezed between Nate and Ethan. "Don't you dare pick up those calls until you answer a question. Did I hear you propose to my sister, Tony, or was that wishful thinking?"

Summer eyed her. "If you were listening at the door, you already know."

"It was noisy in the hallway and I'm not sure."

"I proposed," Tony answered. "And she said yes."

Her sister wooted and did a happy dance, not easy in the limited space.

Tony's crewmates called out congratulations. Then he shooed them away. "Get the heck out of here. My woman needs rest and I'm taking her home—after I drive the aid car back to the station and pick up the CX."

When his buds and her family left, he helped her off the table. "Can you walk by yourself?"

"I could, but maybe I don't want to."

She smiled brightly, this woman he loved. With their arms around each other's waists, they headed toward their future.

THE END

THANK you for letting me share my stories with you!

IF YOU ENJOYED **MR. JULY**, help others find this book by recommending it to your friends and by writing a review. If you would like to know when my next release is available and other fun stuff, sign up for my newsletter here: www.annroth.net

THERE ARE 12 sexy firefighter books planned for the **Heroes of Rogue Valley: Calendar Guys**

OTHER BOOKS:
    Halo Island:
    All I Want for Christmas
    The Pilot's Woman

Ooh, Baby!

ANN ROTH CLASSICS:
Father of the Year
A Place to Belong
My Sisters
Another Life

VISIT ME AT FACEBOOK FACEBOOK.COM/ANN-ROTHAUTHORPAGE
Follow me onTwitter @Ann_Roth
Email me at ann@annroth.net
Visit my website www.annroth.net

THANKS, and until next time,
Ann